This Book Belongs to

_____

Disney's Storyland Treasury

Disney's Storyland Treasury

Disney PRESS

NEW YORK

Table of Contents

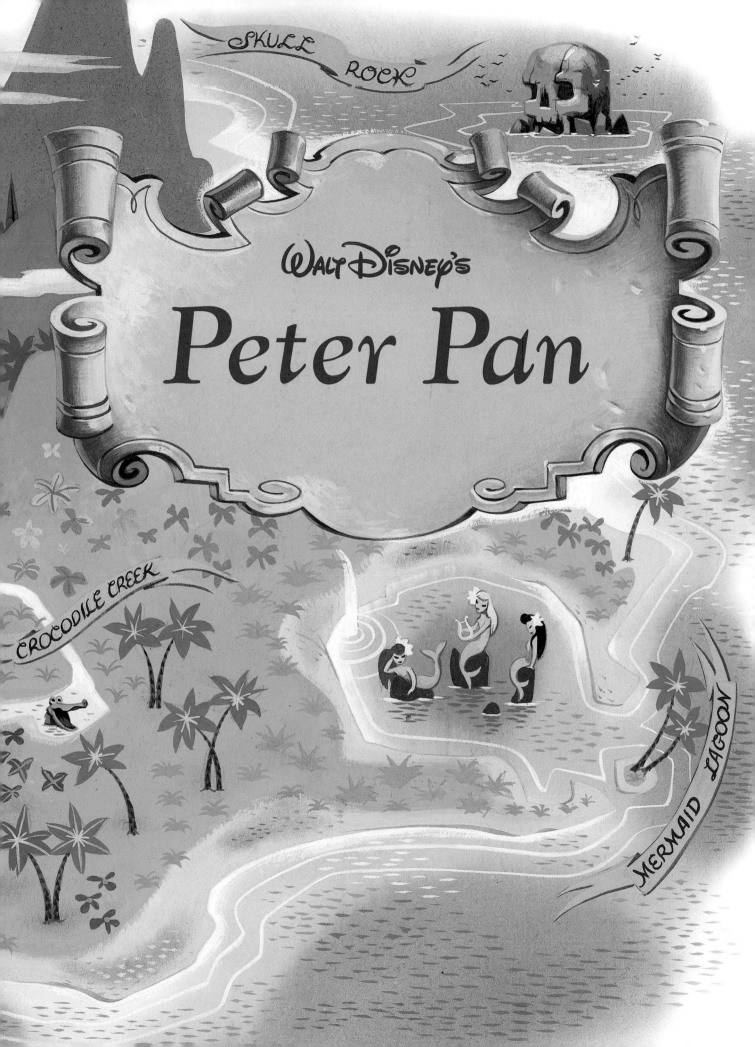

On a quiet street in London lived the Darling family. There was Father and Mother Darling, and Wendy, Michael, and John. There was also the children's nursemaid, Nana—a Saint Bernard dog.

For Nana and the children, the best hour of the day was bedtime, for then they were all together in the nursery. There Wendy told wonderful stories about Peter Pan of Never Land. This Never Land was a magical spot with Indians and mermaids and fairies—and wicked pirates, too.

John and Michael liked best of all to play pirates. They had some fine, slashing duels between Peter Pan and his archenemy, the pirate, Captain Hook.

Father Darling did not like this kind of rough play. He blamed it on Wendy's stories of Peter Pan, and Father Darling did not approve of those stories, either.

"It is time for Wendy to grow up," he said. "This is your last night in the nursery, Wendy girl."

All the children were very upset at that news. Without Wendy in the nursery there would be no more Peter Pan stories! Then, to make matters worse, Father Darling decided there would be no more dogs for nursemaids. The children were very sad indeed. So he tied Nana in the garden for the night.

When Mother and Father Darling had gone out for the evening, leaving the children snug in their beds with Nana on guard below, who should come to the nursery but Peter Pan! It seemed he had been flying in from Never Land all along to listen to the bedtime stories, unseen.

Nana had caught sight of Peter the night before and nipped off his shadow as he had escaped. So back he came, looking for his lost shadow and hoping to hear a story about himself.

With him was a fairy, named Tinker Bell. When Peter heard that Wendy was to be moved from the nursery, he hit upon a plan. "I'll take you to Never Land with me, to tell stories to my Lost Boys!" he exclaimed as Wendy sewed his shadow back on.

Wendy thought that was a lovely idea—but only if Michael and John could go, too. So Peter Pan taught them all to fly—with happy thoughts and faith and trust, and a sprinkling of Tinker Bell's pixie dust. Then out the nursery window they sailed, heading for Never Land, while Nana barked frantically from the ground below.

Back in Never Land, on his pirate ship, Captain Hook was grumbling about Peter Pan. You see, once in a fair fight, long ago, Peter had cut off one of the pirate captain's hands, so that he had to wear a hook in its place. Then Peter threw the hand to a crocodile, who had been lurking around ever since, hoping to nibble at the rest of Hook. Fortunately for the pirate, the crocodile had also swallowed a clock. He went *ticktock, ticktock* all day long, which gave a warning to Captain Hook.

Now, as Captain Hook grumbled about his young enemy, there was a call from the crow's nest.

"Peter Pan, ahoy!"

"What? Where?" shouted Captain Hook, twirling his spyglass up at the sky. And then he spied Peter and the children, pausing for a rest on a cloud. "Swoggle me eyes, it is Pan!" Hook said gloatingly. "Pipe up the crew. . . . Man the guns. . . . We'll get him this time at last!"

"Oh, Peter, it's just as I've dreamed it would be—the Mermaid Lagoon and all," Wendy was saying when the first of the pirates' cannonballs ripped through the cloud close beneath their feet and went sizzling on past.

"Look out!" cried Peter. "Tinker Bell, take Wendy and the boys to the island. I'll stay here and draw Hook's fire!"

Away flew Tinker Bell, as fast as she could go. In her naughty little heart she hoped the children would fall behind and be lost. She was especially jealous of Wendy who seemed to have won Peter Pan's heart.

Straight through the Never Land jungle Tink flew, down into a clearing beside an old dead tree called Hangman's Tree. She landed on a toadstool, bounced to a shiny leaf, and *pop!*, a secret door opened for her in the knot of the hollow tree.

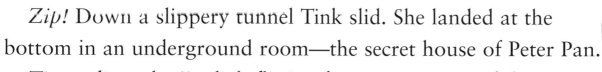

Zip! Down a slippery tunnel Tink slid. She landed at the bottom in an underground room—the secret house of Peter Pan.

Ting-a-ling! she jingled, flitting from one corner of the room to the next. She was trying to awaken the sleeping Lost Boys.

At last, rather grumpily, they woke up and stretched in their little fur suits. And they listened to Tinker Bell.

"What? Peter Pan wants us to shoot down a terrible Wendy bird? Lead us to it!" they shouted, and out they hurried.

When Wendy and Michael and John appeared, flying wearily, the Lost Boys tried to pelt them with stones and sticks—especially the "Wendy bird." Down tumbled Wendy, all her happy thoughts destroyed—for without them no one can fly.

"Hurray! We got the Wendy bird!" the Lost Boys shouted.

But then Peter Pan arrived. How angry he was when he discovered that the boys had tried to shoot down Wendy, even though he had caught her before she could be hurt.

"I brought her to be a mother to us all and to tell us stories," Peter said.

"All right, men," he announced to the excited boys. "Go and capture some Indians. Come on, Wendy, I'll show you the mermaids."

So Peter and Wendy flew away, and the boys marched off through the forest, hopping over rocks and singing through the fields. There were wild animals all around, but the boys never thought to be afraid, until they spotted footprints.

"First we must surround them!" John cried, trying his very best to be a worthy leader. "Then we'll take them by surpri—!"

WHOOP! The Never Land Indians ambushed the boys and carried them away to their camp.

The boys thought their capture was only a game—but the chief was furious. He thought they had kidnapped his daughter.

"Don't worry, the Indians are our friends," the Lost Boys said, but the Indian Chief looked very stern.

Meanwhile, on the other side of the island, Wendy and Peter were visiting the mermaids in their peaceful Mermaid Lagoon. As they were chatting together, Peter suddenly said, "Hush!"

A boat from the pirate ship was going by. In it was the wicked Captain Hook and Smee, the pirate cook. And at the stern, bound with ropes, sat Princess Tiger Lily, the Indian Chief's daughter.

"We'll make her talk," Captain Hook said with a sneer. "She'll tell us where Pan lives, or we'll leave her tied to slippery Skull Rock, where the tide will wash over her."

But proud and loyal Tiger Lily would not say a single word.

Peter and Wendy flew to Skull Rock. Peter imitated Hook's voice, and tried to trick Smee into setting Tiger Lily free. That almost worked, but Hook discovered the trick, and came after Peter with his sword. Then, what a thrilling duel they had, all over that rocky cave where Princess Tiger Lily sat, with the tide up to her chin!

Peter won the duel and rescued Tiger Lily just in the nick of time. Away he flew to the Indian village, to see the princess safely home. And Wendy came along, too.

When Peter and Wendy brought Tiger Lily back, the Indian Chief set the captives all free. Then, what a wonderful feast they had! All the boys did Indian dances and learned wild Indian chants, and Peter Pan was made a chief! Only Wendy had no fun at all, for she had to help the squaws carry firewood.

While the Indian celebration was at its height, Smee crept up through the underbrush and captured Tinker Bell.

Trapped in his cap, she struggled and kicked, but Smee took her back to the pirate ship and presented her to Captain Hook.

"Ah, Miss Bell," said Hook sympathetically, "I've heard how badly Peter Pan has treated you since that scheming girl, Wendy, came along. How nice it would be if we could kidnap her and take her off to sea to scrub the decks and cook for the pirate crew!"

Tink jingled happily at the thought.

"But, alas," said Hook with a sigh, "we don't know where Pan's house is, so we cannot get rid of Wendy for you."

Tink thought this over. "You won't hurt Peter?" she asked, in solemn jingling tones.

"Of course not!" said Hook.

Then Tink marched to a map of Never Land and traced a path to Peter's hidden house.

"Thank you, my dear," said the wicked Captain Hook, and he locked her up in a lantern cage, while he went off to capture Peter Pan!

That night when Wendy tucked the children into their beds in the underground house, she talked to them about home and their mother. Soon they were all so homesick that they wanted to leave at once. Wendy invited all the Lost Boys to come and live with the Darling family. Only Peter refused to go. He simply looked the other way as Wendy and the boys told him good-bye and climbed the tunnel to Hangman's Tree.

Up in the woods near Hangman's Tree waited Hook and his pirate band. As each boy came out, a hand was clapped over his mouth and he was quickly tied up with ropes. Last of all came Wendy. *Zip, zip,* she was bound up, too, and the crew marched off with their load of children, back to the pirate ship.

"Blast it!" muttered Hook. "We still don't have Pan!"

So he and Smee left a wicked bomb, wrapped as a gift from Wendy, for poor Peter to find. Very soon, they hoped, Peter would open it and blow himself straight out of Never Land.

Imagine how terrible Tinker Bell felt when she saw that all the children had been taken prisoner, and knew it was her fault!

The children were given the terrible choice between becoming pirates or walking the plank. To the boys, the life of a pirate sounded fine, sad to say, and they were all ready to join up. But Wendy was shocked. "Never!" she cried.

"Very well," said Hook. "Then you shall be the first to walk the plank, my dear."

Everyone felt so awful—though Wendy was ever so brave—that no one noticed when Tinker Bell escaped and flew off to warn Peter Pan.

What a dreadful moment when Wendy said good-bye and bravely walked out onto the long narrow plank.

And then she disappeared. Everyone listened, breathless, waiting for a splash, but not a single sound came! What could the silence mean?

Then they heard a familiar, happy cry. It was Peter Pan in the rigging, high above. Warned by Tinker Bell, he had escaped just in time to scoop up Wendy in midair and fly with her to safety.

"This time you have gone too far, Hook!" Peter shouted.

He swooped down from the rigging, all set for a duel. And what a duel it was!

While they fought, Tinker Bell slashed the ropes that bound the boys, and they stopped the pirates from jumping overboard and rowing away in their boat. Then Peter knocked Hook's sword overboard, and Hook jumped, too. When the children last saw the evil Captain Hook, he was swimming for the boat, with the crocodile ticktocking hungrily behind him.

Peter Pan took command of the pirate ship. "Heave those
halyards. Up with the jib. We're sailing to London!" he cried.

"Oh, Michael! John!" shouted Wendy. "We're going home!"

And sure enough, with happy thoughts and faith and trust,
and a liberal sprinkling of pixie dust, away flew the pirate ship.
It sailed through the skies till the gangplank reached the Darlings'
nursery windowsill.

But now that they had arrived, the Lost Boys did not want to stay. "We've sort of decided to stick with Peter," they said.

So Wendy, John, and Michael waved good-bye as Peter Pan's ship took off into the sky, carrying the Lost Boys home to Never Land, where they still live today.

Walt Disney's
Santa's Toy Shop

In a land way up north—at the tip of the North Pole—
there's a magical place where winter stays the whole year
long. Elves upon elves zigzag their skis through the snow on
their way to a very special house—the Toy Shop of Mr. and
Mrs. S. Claus.

The warm and cozy house is always filled with mouth-watering smells. In the kitchen, Mrs. Claus and the elves love to make cookies. First, they roll out the dough and cut out each shape. Then they put the cookies in the oven until they bake golden brown.

Santa loves to try the cookies. "Ho, ho, ho!" he
chuckles. "I could eat these all night! But the elves are
in the Toy Shop, preparing for my flight!"

In Santa's Toy Shop, the elves are stitching and sprucing up the last of the dolls. . . .

They're laying out train tracks and painting tunnels
and cars. . . .

They're sawing wooden blocks, making toy parts,
and painting the squares on checkered game boards.

Then, just when the elves finish making each ball, block, truck, marble, and toy . . . they play with them all, to make absolutely sure they're packed with good fun.

Not one detail is missed in Santa's Toy Shop. Santa personally makes sure to paint the very last smile on the very last doll.

Finally, the elves count up all the letters that have come to the North Pole. Then Santa checks his list of names—and checks it once again.

"Boys and girls have written me from all over the world!" Santa smiles and reads aloud.

"A doll for Janie . . . a fire truck for Saul . . . a race car for Nanette . . . and for Jordan, a football! A bike for Nancy . . . new skates for Brett . . . and let's not forget Jerry's train set!"

When Santa is ready to gather all his goods, he opens his
bag big and wide. The elves line up all the toys in the Toy
Shop and send them down the long toy chute . . . one by
one . . . until Santa's bag is filled to the top.

"Tonight is the big night," Santa says. "The biggest
night of the year!"

"Christmas Eve!" chime the elves. "It's finally here!"

"At last, here I go!" says Santa, waving, with a twinkle in his eye. "I must hurry and get the reindeer and pack up my sleigh."

"The elves have done it for you," says Mrs. Claus, waving Santa good night. "Have a great time as you fly around the world tonight."

"Thank you, dear!" shouts Santa with joy. And sure
enough, the elves have packed Santa's sleigh sky-high and
hitched up all the reindeer, who are eager to fly.

So, with a hearty "Ho, ho, ho!" Santa calls out
the name of each reindeer. "And up, up, up we go!"

They fly across the sky and around the whole world,
stopping at the homes of everyone on his list.

Without making a noise (not even a peep!), Santa lands
on the rooftop. Then, with a wink of his eye and a nod of
his head, Santa slips down the chimney as quick as a blink.

Santa loves finding notes . . . and treats of milk and cookies. As he reads each note, he smiles, knowing that he's making wishes come true.

At the very last house, Santa opens his big bag of toys. "At this house, we have a special request," Santa says to his elf. "The children who live here want us to add the Christmas magic that Santa knows best!"

Santa starts with the Christmas tree and adds candy canes, tinsel, ornaments, and lights. For a finish, he tops it with a shining star—big and bright.

He unpacks the electric train and sets up the station. With
a nod of his head, he sends the train racing around the track.

Then, as quick as a flash, he sets up the blocks and flies
the toy plane . . . with that special magic that only Santa has.

As Santa plays with each doll, he sings a final "Noel." And he says, "Now, on Christmas morning the children will see there's Christmas magic in everything—from the tiniest toy to the tip of the tree."

Just before the break of dawn, Santa leaves the very last town. He calls out to his reindeer, "Home to Mrs. Claus by Christmas morning!"

While the children are still dreaming, Santa returns to the North Pole—with his reindeer, elves, and an empty sleigh.

"How was your trip?" asks Mrs. Claus, greeting Santa in the snow.

"Bundles of fun!" replies Santa, with a "Ho, ho, ho!"

Then Santa tells Mrs. Claus all about Christmas Eve—all the chimneys he dropped down, all the letters he read, and the special wish at the very last house.

"And right about now," Santa whispers in her ear, "all the boys and girls are waking up to find out that I've been there!"

When Christmas is over, Santa records all the children in his big book of names. Then he starts thinking about next Christmas, and everything he'll do . . . for each and every boy and girl . . . and especially for you!

Once upon a time, in a faraway land, a lovely queen sat by her window, sewing. As she worked, she pricked her finger with her needle. Three drops of blood fell on the snow-white linen.

How happy I would be if I had a little girl with lips as red as blood, skin as white as snow, and hair as black as ebony, thought the Queen.

When spring came, her wish was granted. A little daughter was born to the Queen, and she was all her mother had desired. But the Queen's happiness was brief. Holding her lovely baby in her arms, she whispered, "Little Snow White!" and then she died.

When the lonely King married again, his new queen was beautiful, but, alas, she was also heartless and cruel. She was jealous of all the lovely ladies in the kingdom, but most jealous of the lovely little princess—Snow White.

Now the evil Queen's most prized possession was a magic mirror. Every day she looked into it and asked:

> *"Magic Mirror on the wall,*
> *Who is the fairest one of all?"*

If the Magic Mirror replied that she was the fairest in the land, all was well. But if another lady was named, the Queen flew into a terrible rage.

As the years passed, Snow White grew more and more beautiful, and her sweet nature made everyone love her— everyone but the Queen.

The Queen's chief fear was that Snow White might grow up to be the fairest in the land. So she banished the young princess to the servants' quarters, made her dress in rags, and forced her to work from morning to night.

But while she worked, Snow White dreamed dreams of a handsome prince who would come someday and carry her off to his castle in the clouds. And as she dusted and scrubbed—and dreamed—Snow White grew more beautiful day by day.

At last came the day the Queen had been dreading. She asked:

> *"Magic Mirror on the wall,*
> *Who is the fairest one of all?"*

And the Magic Mirror replied:

> *"Her lips blood red, her hair like night,*
> *Her skin like snow, her name—Snow White!"*

Pale with anger, the Queen rushed from the room and called the Huntsman to her.

"Take the princess into the forest and bring back her heart in this jeweled box," she said sternly.

The Huntsman bowed his head in grief. He had no choice but to obey the cruel Queen's commands.

Snow White had no fear of the kindly Huntsman. She went happily into the forest with him. It was beautiful there among the trees, and the princess, not knowing what was in store for her, skipped along beside the Huntsman, stopping to pick violets and singing a happy tune.

At last, the poor Huntsman could bear it no longer. He fell to his knees before the princess.

"I cannot kill you, Princess," he said, "even though it is the Queen's command. Run into the forest and hide, and never return to the castle."

Then away went the Huntsman. On his way back to the castle, he killed a small animal and took its heart in the jeweled box to the wicked Queen.

Alone in the forest, Snow White wept with fright. Deeper and deeper into the woods she ran, half blinded by tears. It seemed to her that the roots of trees reached up to trip her, and that branches grabbed at her dress as she passed.

At last, weak with terror, Snow White fell to the ground and lay there, sobbing her heart out.

Ever so quietly, out from burrows and nests and hollow trees, crept the little woodland animals. Bunnies and chipmunks, and raccoons and squirrels gathered around to keep watch over her.

When Snow White looked up and saw them there, she smiled through her tears. At the sight of her smile, the little animals crept closer, snuggling in her lap or nestling in her arms. The birds sang their sweetest melodies, and the little forest clearing was filled with joy.

"I feel ever so much better now," Snow White told her new friends, "but I still do need a place to sleep."

One of the birds chirped something, and the little animals nodded in agreement. Then away flew the birds, leading the way. The bunnies, chipmunks, raccoons, and squirrels scampered after them, and Snow White followed.

At last, through a tangle of brush, Snow White saw a tiny cottage nestled in a clearing up ahead.

"How sweet!" she cried. "It's just like a doll's house." Snow White clapped her hands in delight.

Skipping across a little bridge to the house, Snow White peeked in through one windowpane. There seemed to be no one at home, but the sink was piled high with cups and saucers and plates, which looked as if they had never been washed. Dirty little shirts and wrinkled little trousers hung over chairs, and everything was blanketed with dust.

"Maybe the children who live here have no mother," said Snow White, "and need someone to take care of them. Let's clean their house and surprise them."

So in she went, followed by her forest friends. Snow White found an old broom in the corner and swept the floor, while the little animals did their best to help.

Then Snow White washed all the crumpled little clothes, and set a kettle of delicious soup to bubbling on the hearth.

"Now," she said to the animals, "let's see what is upstairs."

Upstairs they found seven little beds in a row.

"Why, they have their names carved on them," said Snow White. "Doc, Happy, Sneezy, Dopey—such funny names for children! Grumpy, Bashful, Sleepy! My, I'm a little sleepy myself!"

Yawning, she sank down across the little beds and fell asleep. Quietly, the little animals stole away, and the birds flew out the window. All was still in the little house in the forest.

Seven little men came marching through the woods, singing on their way. As they came in sight of their cottage, they stopped short. Smoke was curling from the chimney, and the door was standing open!

"Look! Someone's in our house!" one cried. "Maybe a ghost—er, a goblin—er, a demon!"

"I knew it," said another, with a grumpy look. "Been warning you for two hundred years something awful was about to happen!"

At last, on timid tiptoe, in they went.

"Someone's stolen our dishes," growled the grumpy one.

"No, they're hidden in the cupboard," said Happy with a grin. "But, hey! My cup's been washed! Sugar's all gone!"

At that moment, a sound came from upstairs. It was Snow White yawning and turning in her sleep.

"It's up there—the goblin—er, demon—er, ghost!" exclaimed one Dwarf.

Shouldering their pickaxes, up the stairs they went, seven frightened little Dwarfs.

Standing in a row at the foot of their beds, they stared at the sleeping Snow White.

"Wh—what is it?" whispered one.

"It's mighty purty," said another.

"Why, bless my soul, I think it's a girl!" said a third.

And then Snow White woke up. "Why, you're not children!" she exclaimed. "You're little men. Let me see if I can guess your names." And she did—all of them.

"Supper is not quite ready," said Snow White. "You'll have just enough time to wash."

"Wash!" cried the little men, with horror in their voices. They hadn't washed for, oh, it seemed hundreds of years. But out they marched when Snow White insisted. And it was worth it in the end. For such a supper they had never tasted. Nor had they ever had such an evening of fun. All the forest folk gathered around the cottage windows to watch them play and dance and sing.

Meanwhile, back at the castle, the Huntsman had presented to the wicked Queen the box which, she thought, held Snow White's heart.

"Aha!" she cried. "At last!" And down the castle corridors she hurried straight to the Magic Mirror and she asked:

"*Magic Mirror on the wall,*
Who is the fairest one of all?"

But the Magic Mirror replied:

"*With the Seven Dwarfs will spend the night*
The fairest in the land, Snow White."

Then the Queen realized that the Huntsman had tricked her. She flung the jeweled box at the Magic Mirror, shattering the glass into a thousand pieces. Then, shaking with rage, the Queen hurried down to a dark cave below the palace where she worked her black magic.

First, she disguised herself as a toothless old woman dressed in tattered rags. Then, she searched through her books of magic spells for a horrid spell to cast on Snow White.

"What shall it be?" she muttered to herself. "The poisoned apple, the Sleeping Death? Perfect!"

In a great kettle she stirred up a poison brew. Then she dipped an apple into it—one, two, three times—and the apple came out a beautiful rosy red, the most tempting apple you could hope to see.

Cackling with wicked pleasure, the Queen dropped her poisoned apple into a basket of fruit and started on her journey to the home of the Seven Dwarfs.

She felt certain that her plan would succeed, for the magic spell of the Sleeping Death could be broken only by Love's First Kiss.

And the Queen was certain that no one would find Snow White, asleep in that great forest.

It was morning when the Queen reached the great forest, close to the Dwarfs' cottage. From her hiding place she saw Snow White saying good-bye to the Seven Dwarfs as they marched off to work.

"Now, be careful!" they warned her. "Watch out for the Queen." And Snow White promised that she would.

But when the poor, ragged old woman carrying a basket of apples appeared outside her window, Snow White never thought to be afraid. She gave the old woman a drink of water and spoke to her kindly.

"Thank you, my dear," the Queen cackled. "Now, in return, won't you have one of my beautiful apples?" And she held out the poisoned fruit to Snow White.

Down swooped the little birds and animals, pecking and clawing at the wicked Queen. But still Snow White did not understand. "Stop it!" she cried. "Shame on you." Then she took the poisoned apple and bit into it, and fell down lifeless on the cottage floor.

Away went the frantic birds and animals into the woods to warn the Seven Dwarfs. Now, the Dwarfs had decided among themselves not to do their regular jobs that day. Away at their mine, they were hard at work making a special gift for Snow White.

They looked up in surprise as the birds and animals crowded around them. At first, they did not understand. Then, they realized that Snow White must be in danger. "The Queen!" they cried, and they ran for home.

They were too late. They came racing into the clearing just in time to see the Queen slip away into the shadows. They chased her through the gloomy woods until she plunged into a bottomless gulf and disappeared forever. But that did not bring Snow White back to life.

When the Dwarfs returned home, they found Snow White lying

on the floor as if asleep. They built her a bed of crystal and gold, and set it up in the forest. There they kept watch, night and day.

After a time, the handsome Prince of a nearby kingdom heard travelers tell of the lovely princess asleep in the forest, and he rode there to see her. At once he knew that he loved her truly, so he knelt beside her and kissed her lips.

At the touch of Love's First Kiss,
Snow White awoke. There, bending over her,
was the Prince of her dreams. Snow White
knew that she loved him, too. She said
good-bye to the Seven Dwarfs and, on a white
horse, rode off with the Prince to his Castle
of Dreams Come True.

Walt Disney's
Babes in Toyland

One day, Mary Contrary found a poster from the Toymaker in Toyland. It read:

WANTED: HELPER TO MAKE TOYS. URGENT.

So Mary, her friend Tom Piper, and her younger brothers and sisters wandered along the edge of the Forest of No Return in search of Toyland. Wee Willie Winkie stopped to ask the trees if they knew where the Toymaker lived. But all they did was shake their leaves and rattle their branches.

Finally, they came to a clearing. "I think we've found it," said Tom.

Underneath their feet, the grass gave way to a stone path lined with scented wildflowers. Across the bridge, the children heard the welcoming *ta-ta-ta* of the toy soldiers' trumpets.

Little Boy Blue had never seen such a spectacular sight. "Look, Bo Peep—ice-cream-cone towers and candy-cane columns. Do you think they're good enough to eat?" he said.

"There's only one way to find out—let's go!" exclaimed Bo Peep.

They ran past the clowns and the blocks marked *T*, past the toy-soldier guards and the golden flagpole with the Toyland flag flapping in the breeze.

From the front steps of the great door, the Toymaker's floppy-eared watchdog lifted his head and let out a *ruff-ruff-ruff*!

But by the time they reached the front door, everything seemed strangely quiet. The soldiers had stopped trumpeting, the dog had stopped barking, and even the birds had stopped singing. The sign on the door told them everything they needed to know. "Perhaps he doesn't need our help, after all," said Mary with a sigh.

TOYLAND
TOY FACTORY
CLOSED
for
ALTERATIONS
Business
is not as usual
GENIUS AT WORK
INSIDE

Meanwhile, deep inside the Toy Factory, the Toymaker was hard at work worrying because he didn't have any toys.

"Your troubles will soon be over," his assistant, Grumio, reassured him. "My new invention will put Toyland back in business." Grumio led the Toymaker toward a big object hidden underneath a large, blue cover.

"Well . . . er . . . all right," the Toymaker finally agreed. "I suppose it can't hurt to take a peek."

"From this point forward, you can forget about drawing plans, or painting faces, or tightening screws, or hammering nails," announced Grumio.

"Have you found someone to help us?" asked the Toymaker.

"We won't need anyone's help—my fabulous toy-making machine will do it all!" Grumio declared.

The *ticktock, ticktock* of the clock echoed against the walls of the large room.

"Oh, my goodness!" moaned the Toymaker. "It's half past October. That gives us—"

"Exactly two and a half months until Christmas," said Grumio with a grin. "More than enough time."

The Toymaker raised his eyebrow. "Are you sure?"

"I'm absolutely, positively certain," Grumio assured him.

"My latest concept in automation will totally amaze you," Grumio said eagerly.

"Hmm." The Toymaker rubbed his chin, thinking about all of his poor assistant's half-baked ideas. Grumio was so much better at making messes than making machines.

"Here's the moment you've been waiting for!" exclaimed Grumio, yanking the big, blue cover away.

"Just wait until you see this." Grumio smiled as he reached into his pocket. He pulled out some yellow string, a bit of lace, a strand of ribbon, and a bow.

START

"I simply toss these items into my marvelous toy-making machine . . . add a dash of sugar and a little bit of spice . . . and pull the START switch."

The engine churned, the wheels turned. The machine sputtered and rattled, and hummed and drummed.

Then, in no time at all . . . out popped a perfectly made doll.
"Remarkable!" exclaimed the Toymaker. "Grumio, this is simply
astonishing! Now it looks like we'll be able to make our Christmas
deadline, after all."

"That's only the beginning," said Grumio. One by one, he dropped bits of this and dabs of that into his machine. . . .

And out came dollhouses with pink window shades, and floppy clowns for circus parades,

windup mice with fuzzy felt ears,

balls and bats for baseball cheers,

many a jigsaw-puzzle piece,

party hats with
feathers and fleece,

every letter of the alphabet,

and a supersonic rocket jet.

"Grumio, you're a genius!" the Toymaker cheered.
He decorated his assistant with ribbons and badges.
"You shall be Toyland's most honored citizen."

"Mmm-hmm." Grumio swelled with pride.

"And we'll make millions of trinkets and bears,"
said the Toymaker, "drums and dolls, ships and . . ."

"Yes." Grumio smiled proudly, agreeing with
everything the Toymaker said.

". . . and balls and blocks and railroad trains!" the Toymaker continued as he dashed to the machine, bursting with ideas. He pulled every lever, flipped every switch, pushed every button, twisted every knob, and turned every crank. Down the chute he tossed springs and bolts, jars of paint, patterns and plans, and ribbons and lace.

Lights started flashing, wheels started spinning, and bells started ringing.

But Grumio was too busy counting his awards to notice what the Toymaker was doing.

Suddenly, the machine's horns started honking, and sirens started to blare.

"Wait!" Grumio shouted. "Mr. Toymaker, you're overloading it, sir! You can only make one toy at a time."

But Grumio's warning came too late.

The big toy-making machine began to sputter. It began to hiss.

Then it began to spit out nuts and bolts and springs and bits. Lightbulbs burst and set off sparks. Then . . .

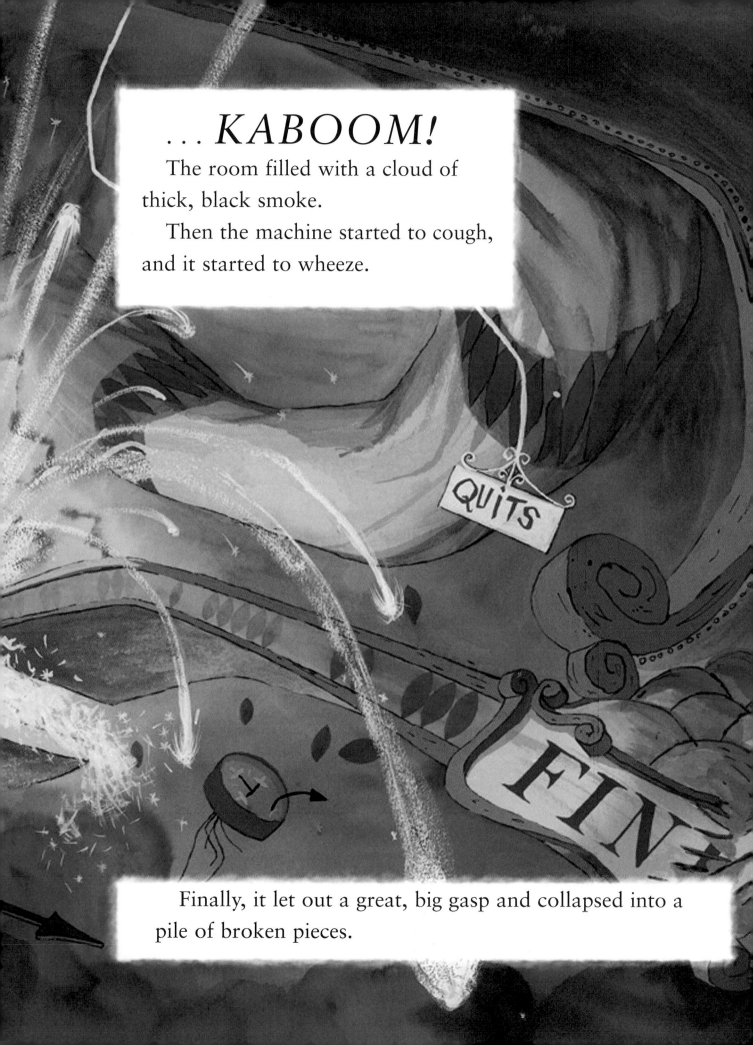

...*KABOOM!*
The room filled with a cloud of
thick, black smoke.
Then the machine started to cough,
and it started to wheeze.

Finally, it let out a great, big gasp and collapsed into a
pile of broken pieces.

Meanwhile, at the edge of Toyland, Tom, Mary, and all her brothers and sisters had given up hope of helping the Toymaker. Sadly, they trod toward the Forest of No Return. But the toy-making machine's powerful explosion shook the entire land.

"The Toymaker really does need our help!" cried Mary. The children ran back across the cobblestone bridge, *clippety, clippety, clippety*, past the toy-soldier guards, and past the Toyland flagpole. The front door swung open wide and welcomed the children inside.

They ran toward the wailing sounds of the sobbing Toymaker. "Whatever will I do now?" he cried.

"We've come to help," explained Tom. "We've come all the way from Mother Goose Village, where we saw your poster."

"What! *Children?*" declared the Toymaker. "I can't possibly allow you to help me. Don't you know that children should never be allowed to see toys before Christmas?"

"But if we don't help you, there won't be any toys at all this year," said Mary.

The Toymaker scratched his head and thought for a moment. "Hmm, I suppose you're right." He nodded. "Then let's get started. Time's a-wasting!"

So the Toymaker whisked the children away to every corner of the factory where he kept all his toy parts, paints, and secret supplies.

Little Boy Blue discovered mountains of buttons and sewed them on teddy bears for noses and eyes.

Wee Willie Winkie sang lullaby songs as he tacked the rockers onto rocking horses and chairs.

Bo Peep took baskets of thread and sewed doll clothes, and puppets, and beanbag toys.

Tom found boxes of every size and shape for every finished toy.

Mary wrapped the gifts in brightly colored paper and festive silk bows.

The Toymaker, happier than ever, put the finishing touches on every last present. He attached handwritten cards that read:

DON'T OPEN TILL CHRISTMAS.

And when all the work was done, Grumio came out with his best invention of all—handpicked, hand-squeezed Pink Lemonade Supreme.

"I made these from the finest pink lemons that Toyland has to offer." Grumio smiled as he poured glasses of the delicious drink for everyone.

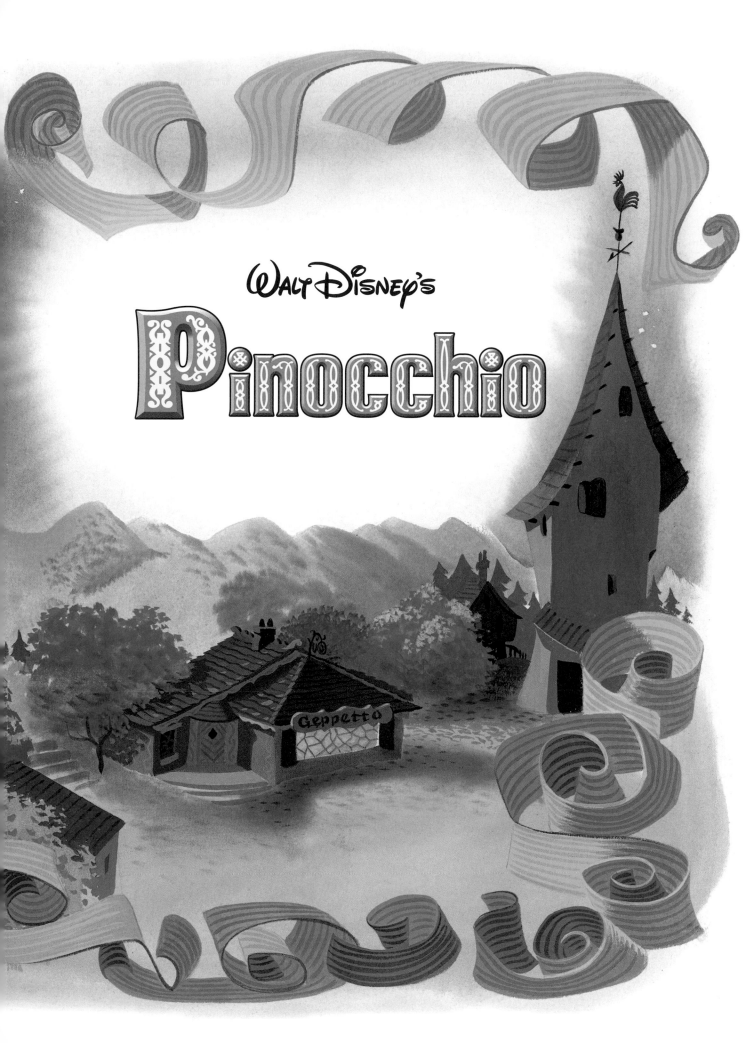

Walt Disney's

Pinocchio

One night, long, long ago, the Evening Star shone down across the dark sky. Its beams formed a shimmering pathway to a tiny village, whose humble little homes lay deep in sleep. Only one house still had a light burning in the window, and that was the workshop of Geppetto, the kindly old wood-carver.

Geppetto had stayed up to finish a merry-faced little puppet he was carving. Now he held the puppet up. "Look, Figaro! Look, Cleo!" he said with a chuckle. "Isn't Pinocchio almost like a real boy?"

The only answer was a snore. Figaro had his soft kitten nose folded into his paws, and Cleo lay sleeping in her goldfish bowl.

"Sleepyheads!" The old wood-carver sighed. Climbing into bed, he mumbled, "I wish you were a real boy, Pinocchio!"

Somebody overheard Geppetto's wish, and that was Jiminy Cricket. All evening Jiminy had sat hidden behind the hearth. He had seen how kind and gentle the wood-carver was, and he felt sorry for him because he knew the lonely old man's wish could never come true.

Suddenly, a shimmering light filled the room. Jiminy gasped. Out of the light stepped a beautiful lady dressed in shining blue. She raised her wand and said, "Wake, Pinocchio! Skip and run! Good Geppetto needs a son!"

Pinocchio blinked his eyes and raised his wooden arms.

"I can move!" he cried. "I'm a real boy!"

"No," the Blue Fairy said sadly. "You have life, but to become a real boy, you must prove yourself brave, truthful, and unselfish."

"But how can I do that?" asked Pinocchio, discouraged.

"You'll have a conscience to help you!" Looking around, the Blue Fairy beckoned Jiminy out of his hiding place. "*Sir* Jiminy Cricket," she said, "I dub you Lord High Keeper of Pinocchio's conscience!"

The next morning, Geppetto couldn't stop rubbing his eyes. There was the puppet he had carved the night before, laughing and chattering and running around the workshop!

"No, no, it can't be true!" Geppetto argued. "It's a dream!"

But Pinocchio ran to him and threw his wooden arms around his neck. "It's true, Father!" he cried. "It's true! I'm alive!"

And then Geppetto realized that a miracle had really happened.

After his first great joy was over, Geppetto said, "But now, Pinocchio, you must go to school." He brought out a bundle of schoolbooks. "Study hard! Then you'll soon become a real boy!"

Pinocchio nodded happily. "Good-bye, Father!" he shouted, and off he marched, his books under his arm, chock-full of good resolutions.

Meanwhile, Jiminy Cricket had overslept and now jumped up
in a great hurry. Quickly, he stuffed his shirt into his trousers and
rushed out. "Hey, Pinoke!" he called. "Wait for me!"

Panting, he caught up with Pinocchio just as the silly little
puppet was walking off arm in arm with the worst pair of scoundrels
in the whole countryside! The villains were a fox by the name of
J. Worthington Foulfellow and a silly cat called Gideon.

"Yes," the sly fox was saying to Pinocchio, "you're too talented
a boy to waste your time in school—isn't he, Gideon?"

Gideon nodded.

"With that face, you should be an actor, my boy!" said Foulfellow.

Pinocchio smiled, pleased at the flattery.

"But, Pinoke!" cried Jiminy. "What will your father say?"

Pinocchio looked startled when he saw Jiminy. He said angrily, "Oh, Father will be proud of me!"

Jiminy knew Pinocchio was being foolish. But the Blue Fairy had appointed him the puppet's conscience, so he followed along loyally.

Soon they came to a marionette theater. When Stromboli, its owner, saw Pinocchio, his small evil eyes glistened. "What a lucky card!" he cried with delight. "A puppet without strings!"

The fox nodded. "And he's yours," he said, smiling greedily and holding out his paw, "for a certain price, of course!"

That night, Pinocchio sang and danced with the spotlight upon him, as Foulfellow the Fox had promised. The audience clapped and cheered and roared for more. A puppet without strings! It was a miracle!

Jiminy, sitting in the audience, felt terrible. *You'd better congratulate Pinocchio and go off . . . alone,* he thought sadly to himself. *What does a great actor need a conscience for?*

After the show, Pinocchio held out his hand to Stromboli and said shyly, "Good-bye, sir, and thank you. Shall I come back tomorrow?"

Stromboli smiled an ugly smile. "Not so fast, young man," he snarled. "You're mine, and you stay here!" And *bang!* before Pinocchio could resist, he was locked inside a birdcage!

When Jiminy came backstage, what a surprise it was to see the great actor in such a position!

"Oh, Jiminy," Pinocchio sobbed, "why didn't I go to school? I'll never see my father again!"

Jiminy tried to pick the lock, but without success. Gloomily, he sat down next to Pinocchio, not even noticing how the room began to glow and grow brighter. Suddenly, the Blue Fairy stood before them!

"I'll help you this time," she said, "because you are truly sorry. But run home now, Pinocchio, and be a good son, or you'll never become a real boy!"

And as she waved her wand, Jiminy and Pinocchio found themselves standing on the open road again!

"Whew!" Pinocchio sighed thankfully. "Let's go home, Jiminy!"

The two friends started running as fast as they could, when whom should they bump into but Foulfellow and Gideon!

"Pinocchio!" Foulfellow cried. "My dearest young friend! How does it feel to be a great actor?"

"Awful!" said Pinocchio. "'Stromboli put me in a cage!" And he told Foulfellow how badly he had fared.

The sly fox pretended to be deeply shocked. And before Jiminy knew what had happened, Foulfellow had persuaded the gullible puppet to forget his good resolutions and take a "rest cure" on Pleasure Island.

"Pinocchio!" Jiminy cried. "You promised to go right home!"

"I will, later on! For now, I need a rest after my terrible experience!" Pinocchio said.

They came to a coach bound for Pleasure Island. It was pulled by small donkeys and filled with rude, noisy boys.

As Pinocchio climbed aboard, Jiminy saw the sly Coachman slip Foulfellow a heavy bag. Again, the fox had sold Pinocchio!

The Coachman cracked his whip, the boys shouted, and the coach started. The only ones who didn't seem happy were Jiminy and the small donkeys.

After boarding a ferry, the coach and its passengers soon docked at Pleasure Island. The boys piled down the gangplank and into the streets. Here there were bands playing, streets paved with cookies and lined with doughnut trees, and fountains spouting lemonade. The Coachman kept urging the boys, "Have a good time—while you can!"

And they did! They climbed the ice-cream mountains and sailed down the lemonade river. They smashed windows, burned schoolbooks, and teased the poor little donkeys. Pinocchio made friends with the very worst of the boys, a mischievous bully named Lampwick.

One day, down on Tobacco Lane, Jiminy came upon Pinocchio puffing on a corncob pipe. Lampwick had a big cigar. Jiminy lost his temper and shouted, "This has gone far enough! Throw away that pipe and come home this minute!"

Pinocchio looked sheepish, but Lampwick began to snicker. "Don't tell me you're scared of a *beetle*!" he said insultingly.

"Gosh, no, Lampwick. That's only Jiminy. He can't tell me what to do!" And right in Jiminy's face, Pinocchio blew a puff of smoke!

Jiminy was about to march off angrily when suddenly Lampwick grabbed his head, and Pinocchio cried, "Jiminy, my ears are buzzing!"

Before Jiminy's shocked eyes, the boys were sprouting donkey ears!

"It's donkey fever!" whispered Jiminy, horrified. "You were lazy, good-for-nothing boys, so now you're turning into donkeys. Let's get out of here!" Quickly, they dashed through the strangely deserted streets.

As they rounded a corner, they came face-to-face with the Coachman. He and armed guards were herding a bunch of braying, howling donkeys, many of which still wore boys' hats and shoes.

"There they go! Those are the two that are missing!" yelled the Coachman. "After them!"

Bullets whizzed past them as they rushed toward the wall surrounding the island. Pinocchio and Jiminy managed to scramble up, but when they looked down, they saw a little donkey dressed in Lampwick's clothes. It *was* Lampwick.

"Go on, Pinocchio!" Lampwick cried. "It's all over for me!"

There was nothing they could do. Sadly, Pinocchio followed Jiminy and dove into the sea.

They had a long, hard swim to the mainland, and a longer, harder journey home. It was winter in the village, and through the drifting snow they hurried to Geppetto's door and pounded on it. The only answer they heard was the howling of the wintry wind. Pinocchio peered into the window. The house was empty!

"My father's gone away!" said Pinocchio, and a tear ran down his long nose and froze into a tiny, sparkling icicle.

Just then, a gust of wind blew a piece of paper around the corner. "Hey, Pinoke!" Jiminy exclaimed. "It's a letter!"

The little cricket began to read the note aloud:

"Dear Pinocchio:

   "I heard you had gone to Pleasure Island, so Figaro, Cleo, and I
started off in a small boat to find you. Just as we came in sight of
the island, out of the sea rose Monstro, the giant whale. He
opened his jaws and in we went. Now, dear son, we are living in
the belly of the whale. But there is very little to eat here, and we
cannot exist much longer, so I fear you will never again see me.

"Your loving father,

"GEPPETTO"

For a while, both Jiminy and Pinocchio were silent, too upset to
speak. Then, in a resolute voice that Jiminy had never heard him
use before, Pinocchio said, "I am going to save my father!"

"But Pinocchio," cried Jiminy, "think how far it is to the ocean!"

"I don't mind," Pinocchio said firmly. "I must find Father."

Just then a soft voice said, "I will take you." And out of the sky fluttered a small white dove with a golden crown on its head.

Pinocchio stared. "You?" he asked. "How could *you* carry us?"

"Like this!" said the dove as she began to grow and grow. "Climb on," she commanded, and off they went. All day and all night they flew, until they reached the high cliffs of the seashore.

They landed. "Good-bye!" called the dove. "Good luck!" And she flew away. Pinocchio and Jiminy did not know that she was their very own Blue Fairy in disguise, and that it was she who had brought them Geppetto's letter.

Then, Pinocchio tied a big stone to his donkey tail. He smiled bravely at Jiminy, and together they leaped off the cliff into the roaring ocean below.

Down, down, down they went, through the green water, past clumps of waving seaweed. At the sandy bottom, Pinocchio scrambled to his feet. "Come on," he said. "Let's find Monstro the Whale." He started off, peering into every grotto and green sea cave.

"We'll never find him," muttered Jiminy.

Jiminy was wrong. Very near them floated the whale they were looking for, fast asleep. Inside the whale, at the far end of its mouth's dark cavern, Geppetto had set up a strange household. He had salvaged a decrepit home from the ships that the whale had swallowed, and every day he fished in the whale's mouth. But now that Monstro was sleeping, no fish came in.

"Not a bite for days, Figaro," Geppetto said mournfully. "If Monstro doesn't wake soon, we'll all starve."

Geppetto sighed and continued fishing. With his ribs nearly piercing his fur, Figaro began to sneak greedily toward Cleo's bowl.

But Geppetto saw him. "Scat!" he shouted. "Shame on you!"

Just then, Geppetto felt a nibble. "Food, Figaro!" he cried. But when the catch was landed, it was only a cookbook on *101 Ways to Cook Fish*.

Geppetto turned the pages, his mouth watering. Slowly his eyes were drawn to Cleo. Moving as if he were in a nightmare, Geppetto started to scoop her out of her bowl. But as he was about to drop her in the frying pan, he realized that he could never really eat his little pet.

"Dear Cleo," he begged, "forgive me!"

It was a solemn moment. They all felt that the end was near.

And then the whale moved!

Monstro gave an upward lunge, and through his jaw rushed a wall of black water. With it came a whole school of tuna!

Nearby, Pinocchio saw the sea creatures fleeing. He caught a glimpse of Monstro coming toward him. Then he, too, was sucked down through those huge jaws.

Bobbing up and down in an empty bottle, Jiminy begged to be swallowed, too. But Monstro just went back to sleep.

Meanwhile, Geppetto was pulling fish after fish out of the water. "Food!" he yelled. "Oh, Figaro, Cleo—we are saved!"

He was so busy, he scarcely heard a shrill cry of "Father!"

"Pinocchio?" he asked wonderingly, and turned around. "Oh, my own dear son!" he exclaimed. "Is it really you?"

With tears in his eyes, the old man embraced Pinocchio. But when he lovingly took off his son's hat, out popped the dreadful donkey ears.

Pinocchio turned his face away in shame. "I've got a tail, too," he admitted sadly. "Oh, Father!"

"Never mind, son," Geppetto said comfortingly. "The main thing is that we are all together again."

"And that we get out of here," Pinocchio added.

"We never will. I've tried everything . . . I even built a raft. . . ."

"That's it!" cried Pinocchio. "When Monstro opens his mouth, we'll float out on that raft."

"Oh, no," argued Geppetto. "When Monstro opens his mouth, everything comes in—nothing goes out."

"Yes," said Pinocchio thoughtfully, "that is, if he swallows. But not . . . not if he sneezes! Quick, Father, help me build a fire!"

Before Geppetto knew what he was doing, Pinocchio set fire to a pile of chairs and crates that he had quickly tossed together.

As the fire began to smoke, they got the raft ready. The whale grunted. Suddenly, he drew in his breath and gave a monstrous *SNEEZE*! Out went the raft into the open sea!

But they were still not free. The angry whale saw them and plunged after them. With one blow he splintered their frail craft.

Geppetto felt himself sinking. "My son, save yourself!" he cried.

But the brave puppet swam to him and kept him afloat. Giant waves swept them toward dark rocks looming against the shore. Just as they were about to be crushed against the rocks, they were washed through a tiny crevice into a lagoon. In vain, Monstro hurled his bulk against the other side. His prey had escaped!

Geppetto lay on the beach, gratitude filling his heart. Then he saw Pinocchio lying beside him—still, cold, and pale!

A fishbowl floated up to the water's surface. A bedraggled kitten clung to the edge of the bowl, and beside it bobbed Jiminy Cricket in his bottle.

But neither Cleo, Figaro, nor Jiminy could comfort the heartbroken old man as he wept bitterly, sure that his wooden boy was dead.

The old man gathered poor Pinocchio into his arms and started home. When he reached his cottage, he sank down and prayed.

Suddenly, a ray of starlight pierced the gloom. A soft voice said, as it had said once before, "And someday, when you have proved yourself brave, truthful, and unselfish, you will become a real boy. . . ."

Pinocchio stirred and sat up. He looked at himself and felt his arms and legs. Then he knew!

"Father!" he cried joyfully. "Father! Look at me!"

The Blue Fairy's promise had come true! Pinocchio was no longer a puppet! Pinocchio was a real, live, flesh-and-blood boy!

Once upon a time in a far-off land, there lived a kindly gentleman. He had a fine home and a lovely little daughter, and he gave her all that money could buy—a pony of her own, a funny puppy dog, and beautiful dresses to wear.

But the little girl had no mother. She longed for a mother and for other children to play with. So her father married a woman with two daughters. Now, with a new mother and sisters, he thought, his little daughter had everything to make her happy.

But, alas, the kindly gentleman soon died. His fine home fell into disrepair. And his second wife was harsh and cold. She cared only for her own two ugly daughters. To her lovely stepdaughter she was cruel as cruel could be.

Everyone called the stepdaughter "Cinderella" now. For she had to work hard, she was dressed in rags, and she sat by the cinders to keep herself warm. Her horse grew old, locked up in the barn. And her dog was not allowed in the house.

But do you suppose Cinderella was sad? Not a bit! She made friends with the birds who flew to her windowsill. She became friends with the barnyard chickens and geese. And her best friends of all were—guess who?—the mice!

The musty old house was full of mice. Their homes were in the garret, where Cinderella lived. She made little clothes for them, and gave them all names. And they thought Cinderella was the sweetest, most beautiful girl in the world.

Every morning, Cinderella's friends the mice and birds woke her from her dreams. Then, it was breakfast time for the household— with Cinderella doing all the work, of course. Out on the back steps she set a bowl of milk for the Stepmother's disagreeable cat, who watched for his chance to catch the mice. The faithful dog had a tasty bone. There was grain for the chickens and ducks and geese. And Cinderella gave some grain to the mice—when they were out of reach of the cat, of course. Then, back into the house she went.

Up the long stairway she carried breakfast trays for her stepmother and her two lazy stepsisters. And down she came with a basket of mending, some clothes to wash, and a long list of jobs to do for the day.

"Now let me see," her stepmother would say. "You can clean the large carpet in the main hall. And wash all the windows, upstairs and down. Scrub the terrace. Sweep the stairs—and then you may rest."

"Oh," said Cinderella. "Yes." And off to work she went.

Now across the town from Cinderella's home was the palace of the King. And in the King's study one day sat the King himself, giving orders to the Grand Duke. "The Prince must marry!" exclaimed the King. "It is high time!"

"But, Your Majesty, what can we do?" asked the Grand Duke. "First, he must fall in love."

"We can arrange that," said the King. "We shall give a great ball, this very night, and invite every girl in the land!"

There was great excitement in Cinderella's home when the invitations to the King's ball arrived.

"How delightful!" the stepsisters said to each other. "We are going to the palace to a ball!"

"And I—" said Cinderella, "—I am invited, too!"

"Oh, you!" The stepsisters laughed.

"Yes, you!" mocked the Stepmother. "Of course you may go, if you finish your work," she said. "And if you have something suitable to wear. I said *if*." And she smiled a horrid smile.

Cinderella worked as hard as she could, all the long day. But when it was time to leave for the ball, she had not a moment to fix herself up, or to give a thought to a dress.

"Why, Cinderella, you are not ready," said the Stepmother, when the coach was at the door.

"No, I am not going," said Cinderella sadly.

"Not going! Oh, what a shame!" the Stepmother said with her mocking smile. "But there will be other balls."

Poor Cinderella! She went to her room and sat down sadly, with her head in her hands.

But a twittering sound soon made her turn around. Her little friends had not forgotten her. They had been scampering and flying about, fixing a party dress for her.

"Oh, how lovely!" she cried. "I can't thank you enough," she told all the birds and the mice. She looked out the window. The coach was still there. So she started to dress for the ball.

"Wait!" cried Cinderella. "I am coming, too!"

She ran down the long stairway just as the Stepmother was giving her daughters some last commands. At the sound of Cinderella's voice, they all turned and stared.

"My beads!" cried one stepsister.

"And my ribbon!" cried the other, snatching off Cinderella's sash. "And those bows! You thief! Those are mine!"

So they pulled and they ripped and they tore at the dress, until Cinderella was in rags once more. And then they flounced off to the ball.

Poor Cinderella! She ran to the garden behind the house. And there, she sank down onto a low stone bench and wept as if her heart would break.

But soon she felt someone beside her. She looked up, and through her tears she saw a sweet-faced little woman. "Oh," said Cinderella. "Good evening. Who are you?"

"I am your fairy godmother," said the little woman. And from the thin air she pulled a magic wand. "Now dry your tears. You can't go to the ball looking like that!

"Let's see now. The first thing you will need is—a pumpkin!"
the Fairy Godmother said.

Cinderella did not understand, but she brought the pumpkin.

"And now for the magic words—*Bibbidi-Bobbidi-Boo!*"
said the Fairy Godmother. Slowly, up reared the pumpkin on its
pumpkin vine, and it turned into a handsome magic coach. "What
we need next are some fine big—mice!"

Cinderella brought her friends the mice. And at the touch of
the wand they turned into prancing horses.

Then the old horse became a fine coachman.

And Bruno, the dog, turned into a footman at the touch of the wand and a *Bibbidi-Bobbidi-Boo!*

"There," said the Fairy Godmother, "now hop in, child. You've no time to waste. The magic only lasts till midnight!"

"But my dress—" Cinderella said, looking at her rags.

"Good heavens, child!" exclaimed the Fairy Godmother. "Of course you can't go in that! *Bibbidi-Bobbidi-Boo!*"

The wand waved again, and there Cinderella stood—in the most beautiful gown in the world, with tiny slippers of glass.

The Prince's ball was underway. The palace was ablaze with light. The ballroom gleamed with silks and jewels. And the Prince smiled and bowed, but still looked bored, as all the young ladies of the kingdom in turn curtsied before him.

Up above on a balcony stood the King and the Grand Duke, looking on. "Whatever is the matter with the Prince?" cried the King. "He doesn't seem to care for any of those beautiful maidens."

"I feared as much," the Grand Duke said with a sigh. "The Prince is not one to fall in love at first sight."

But at that very moment, he did! For just then, Cinderella appeared at the doorway of the ballroom. The Prince caught sight of her through the crowd. And like one in a dream he walked to her side, and offered her his arm.

Quickly, the King beckoned to the musicians, and they struck up a dreamy waltz. The Prince and Cinderella swirled across the dance floor. And the King, chuckling over the success of his plan to find a bride for the Prince, went happily off to bed.

All evening, the Prince was at Cinderella's side. They danced every
dance. They ate supper together. And Cinderella had such a wonderful
time that she quite forgot the Fairy Godmother's warning until the
clock in the palace tower began to strike midnight. *Bong! Bong!*

"Oh!" cried Cinderella. The magic was about to end!

Without a word she ran from the ballroom, down the long palace
hall, and out the door. One of her little glass slippers flew off, but she
could not stop.

She leaped into her coach, and away they raced for home. But as
they rounded the first corner, the clock finished its strokes. The spell
was broken. And there in the street stood an old horse, a dog, and
a girl in rags, staring at a small round pumpkin. Some mice ran
chattering about them.

"Glass slipper!" the mice cried. "Glass slipper!"

And Cinderella looked down. Sure enough, there was a glass slipper on the pavement.

"Oh, thank you, Godmother!" she said.

The next morning there was great excitement in the palace. The King was furious when he found out that the Grand Duke had let the beautiful girl slip away.

"All we could find was this one glass slipper," the Grand Duke admitted. "And now the Prince says he must marry the girl whom this slipper fits. And he will not marry anyone else."

"He did?" cried the King. "He said he would marry her? Well then, find her! Scour the kingdom, and find that girl!"

All day and all night the Grand Duke and his servant traveled about the kingdom, trying to find a foot on which the glass slipper would fit. In the morning, his coach drove up in front of Cinderella's house.

The news of the search had run on ahead, and the Stepmother was busy rousing her ugly daughters and preparing them to greet the Grand Duke. For she was determined that one of them should wear the slipper and be the Prince's bride.

"The Prince's bride," whispered Cinderella. "I must dress, too. The Grand Duke must not find me like this."

Cinderella went off to her room to dress, humming a waltzing tune played at the ball the night before. Then the Stepmother suspected the truth: Cinderella was the girl that the Prince was seeking. So she followed Cinderella—to lock her in her room.

The mice chattered a warning, but Cinderella did not hear them. She was off in a world of dreams.

Then she heard the key click. The door was locked. "Please let me out—oh, please!" she cried. But the wicked Stepmother only laughed and went away.

"We will save you!" said the loyal mice. "We will somehow get that key!"

The household was in a tizzy. The Grand Duke had arrived. His servant held the glass slipper.

"It is mine!" "It is mine!" both stepsisters cried.

And each strained and pushed and tried to force her foot into the tiny glass slipper. But they failed.

Meanwhile, the mice made themselves into a long chain. The mouse at the end dropped down into the Stepmother's pocket. He popped up again with the key to Cinderella's room! At once, the mice hurried off with the key.

Now the Grand Duke was at the door, about to leave. Suddenly, Cinderella came flying down the stairs.

"Oh, wait, wait, please!" she called. "May I try the slipper on?"

"Of course," said the Grand Duke. And he called the servant back with the slipper. But the wicked Stepmother tripped the boy. The slipper fell and—*crash*—it splintered into a thousand pieces. "Oh my, oh my!" said the Grand Duke. "What can I ever tell the King?"

"Never mind," said Cinderella. "I have the other one here." And she pulled the other glass slipper from her pocket!

So off to the palace went Cinderella in the King's own coach, with the happy Grand Duke by her side. The Prince was delighted to see her again. So was his father, the King. And so was everyone. For this sweet and beautiful girl won the hearts of all who met her.

Soon, she was Princess of the land. And she and her husband, the charming Prince, rode to their palace in a golden coach and lived happily ever after!

Bambi

When Bambi was born, the forest animals came to greet him.

Bambi came into the world in the middle of a forest thicket. The little, hidden thicket was scarcely big enough for the new baby and his mother.

But a magpie soon spied him there.

"What a beautiful baby!" she cried. And away she flew to spread the news to all the other animals of the forest.

Her chattering soon brought dozens of birds and animals to the thicket. The rabbits came hurrying; the squirrels came a-scurrying. The robins and bluebirds fluttered and flew.

At last, even the old owl woke up from his long day's sleep.

"Who, who?" the owl said sleepily, hearing all the commotion.

"Wake up, Friend Owl!" a rabbit called. "It's happened! The young prince is born!"

"Everyone's going to see him," said the squirrels. "You must come, too."

With a sigh, the owl spread his wings and flew off toward the thicket. There he found squirrels and rabbits and birds peering through the bushes at a doe and a little spotted fawn.

The fawn was Bambi, the new Prince of the Forest.

"Congratulations," said the owl, speaking for all the animals. "This is quite an occasion. It isn't often that a prince is born in the forest."

The doe looked up. "Thank you," she said quietly. Then with her nose she gently nudged her sleeping baby until he lifted his head and looked around.

She nudged him again, and licked him reassuringly. At last, he pushed up on his thin legs, trying to stand.

"Look! He's trying to stand up already!" shouted one of the little rabbits, named Thumper. "He's awfully wobbly, though, isn't he?"

"Thumper!" the mother rabbit exclaimed, pulling him back. "That's not a pleasant thing to say!"

The new fawn's legs were not very steady, it was true, but at last he stood beside his mother. Now, all the animals could see the fine white spots on his red-brown coat, and the sleepy expression on his soft baby face.

The forest around him echoed with countless small voices. A soft breeze rustled the leaves about the thicket. And the watching animals whispered among themselves. But the little fawn did not listen to any of them. He only knew that his mother's tongue was licking him softly, washing and warming him. He nestled closer to her, and closed his sleepy eyes.

Thumper, the bunny, became Bambi's first friend.

Quietly, the animals and birds slipped away through the forest. Thumper the rabbit was the last to go.

"What are you going to name the young prince?" he asked.

"I'll call him Bambi," the mother answered.

"Bambi," Thumper said. "Bambi. That's a good name. Good-bye, Bambi." And he hopped away after his sisters.

Bambi was not a sleepy baby for long. Soon he was following his mother down the narrow forest paths. Bright flowers winked at him from beneath the leaves. Prickly branches tickled his legs as he passed.

Squirrels and chipmunks looked up and called, "Good morning, young prince."

Opossums, hanging by their long tails from a tree branch, said, "Hello, Prince Bambi."

The fawn looked at them all with wondering eyes. But he did not say a word.

Finally, as Bambi and his mother reached a little clearing in the forest, they met Thumper and his family.

"Hi, Bambi," said Thumper. "Come on and play."

"Yes, let's play!" Thumper's sisters cried. And away they hopped, over branches and hillocks and tufts of grass.

Bambi soon understood the game, and he began to jump and run on his stiff, spindly legs.

Thumper jumped over a log and his sisters followed.

"Come on, Bambi," Thumper called. "Hop over the log."

Bambi jumped, but not far enough. He fell with a plop on top of the log.

"Too bad," said Thumper. "You'll do better next time."

Bambi learned to play games with the bunnies.

Bambi untangled his legs and stood up again. But still he did not speak. He pranced along behind Thumper, and soon he saw a family of birds sitting on a branch.

Bambi looked at them.

"Those are birds, Bambi," Thumper told him. "Birds."

"Bir-d," Bambi said slowly. The young prince had spoken his first word!

Thumper and his sisters were all excited, and Bambi was pleased, too. He repeated the word over and over to himself.

Then he saw a butterfly cross the path. "Bird, bird!" he cried again.

"No, Bambi," said Thumper. "That's not a bird. That's a butterfly."

The butterfly disappeared into a clump of yellow flowers. Bambi bounded toward them happily.

"Butterfly!" he cried.

"No, Bambi," said Thumper. "Not butterfly. *Flower.*"

Thumper pushed his nose into the flowers and sniffed. Bambi did the same, but suddenly he drew back. His nose had touched something warm and furry.

Out from the bed of flowers came a small black and white head with two shining eyes.

"Flower!" cried Bambi.

As the little animal stepped out, the white stripe down his black furry back glistened in the sun.

Thumper was laughing so hard that he could barely speak.

"That's not a flower," said Thumper. "That's a skunk."

"Flower," Bambi said again.

"I don't care," said the skunk. "The young prince can call me Flower if he wants to. I don't mind."

And that's how Flower, the skunk, got his name.

One morning, Bambi and his mother walked down a new path. It grew lighter and lighter as they walked along. Soon the trail ended in a tangle of bushes and vines, and Bambi could see a great, bright, open space spread out before them.

Bambi wanted to bound out there to play in the sunshine, but his mother stopped him. "Wait," she said. "You must never run out on the meadow without first making sure it is safe."

She took a few slow, careful steps forward. She listened and sniffed in all directions. Then she called, "Come."

Bambi ran out. He felt so good and so happy that he leaped into the air again and again. For the meadow was the most beautiful place he had ever seen.

His mother dashed forward and showed him how to race and play in the tall grass. Bambi ran after her. He felt as if he were flying. Round and round they raced in great circles. At last, his mother stopped and stood still, catching her breath.

Bambi saw his own face in a meadow pool.

Then Bambi and his mother set out to explore the meadow. Soon he spied his little friend the skunk, sitting in the shade of some blossoms.

"Good morning, Flower," said Bambi.

Next he found Thumper and his sisters nibbling on some sweet clover.

"Try some, Bambi," said Thumper.

So Bambi did.

Suddenly, a big green frog popped out of the clover patch and hopped over to a meadow pond. Bambi had not seen the pond before, so he hurried over for a closer look.

As the fawn came near, the frog hopped into the water.

Where could he have gone? Bambi wondered. So he bent down to look into the pond. As the ripples cleared, Bambi jumped back. For he saw a fawn down there in the water, looking up at him!

"Don't be frightened, Bambi," his mother said to him. "You are just seeing yourself in the water."

Bambi met another little fawn. Her name was Faline.

So Bambi looked once more. This time he saw *two* fawns looking out at him! He jumped back again, and as he lifted his head, he saw that it was true—there was another little fawn standing beside him!

"Hello," she said.

Bambi backed away and ran to his mother, where she was quietly eating grass beside another doe. Bambi leaned against her and peered out at the other little fawn, who had followed him there.

"Don't be afraid, Bambi," his mother said. "This is little Faline, and this is your Aunt Ena. Can't you say hello to them?"

"Hello, Bambi," said the two deer. But Bambi did not say a word.

"You have been wanting to meet other deer," his mother reminded him. "Well, Aunt Ena and Faline are deer just like us. Now, can't you speak to them?"

"Hello," whispered Bambi in a small, small voice.

"Come and play, Bambi," said Faline. She leaned forward and licked his face.

Bambi dashed away as fast as he could run, and Faline raced after him. They almost flew over the meadow.

Up and down they chased each other. Over the little hillocks they raced.

When they stopped, all topsy-turvy and breathless, they were good friends.

Then they walked side by side on the bright meadow, visiting quietly together.

One morning, Bambi woke up, shivering with cold. Even before he opened his eyes, his nose told him there was something new and strange in the world. Then he looked out of the thicket. Everything was covered with white.

"It is snow, Bambi," his mother said. "Go ahead and walk out. It is all right."

Bambi stepped out onto the snow very cautiously. His feet sank deep into the soft blanket. He had to lift them up high as he walked along. Now and then, with a soft plop, a tiny snowy heap would tumble from a leaf overhead onto his nose or back.

Bambi was delighted. The sun glittered so brightly on the whiteness. The air was so mild and clear. And all around him white snow stars came whirling down.

From the crest of a little hill, he saw Thumper. Thumper was sitting on the top of the pond!

"Come on, Bambi!" Thumper shouted. "Look! The water's stiff!" He thumped with one foot against the solid ice. "You can even slide on it. Watch!"

One day, Bambi awoke to find the world white with snow.

Thumper took a run and slid swiftly across the pond. Bambi tried it, too, but his legs shot out from under him and down he crashed onto the hard ice. That was not so much fun.

"Let's play something else," Bambi suggested, when he had carefully pulled himself to his feet again. "Where's Flower?"

"I think I know," said Thumper.

He led Bambi to the doorway of a deep burrow. They peered down into it. There, peacefully sleeping on a bed of withered flowers, lay the little skunk.

"Wake up, Flower!" Bambi called.

"Is it spring yet?" Flower asked sleepily, half opening his eyes.

"No, winter's just beginning," Bambi said. "What are you doing?"

"Hibernating," the little skunk replied. "Flowers like to sleep in the winter, you know."

Thumper yawned. "I guess I'll take a nap, too," he said. "Good-bye, Bambi. I'll see you later."

So Bambi was left alone. Sadly, he wandered back to the thicket.

"Don't fret, Bambi," his mother said. "Winter will soon be over, and spring will come again."

So Bambi went to sleep beside his mother in the snug, warm thicket, and dreamed of the jolly games that he and his friends would play when springtime came again.

Bambi and his friends would play together in the spring.

NOAH'S ARK

F ather Noah had no time to waste. A flood was coming! God told him to make haste and gather wood, then measure it, cut it, and bind it with pitch.

Birds squawked with excitement and flew through the skies.
"Ark! Ark! Noah's building an ark!" shrieked the magpie.

The birds spread the news to their friends on the African plains. "I've never seen enough rain for a flood," said the rhinoceros with a grunt.

"Listen!" cried the blue jay throughout the Asian highlands.
"Noah is building an ark to save us from a great flood!"

"Impossible!" snarled the tiger.

"God told Noah the rain will fall for forty days and forty nights," chirped the warbler.

"That's all right." The gorilla smiled. "A little rain won't bother me at all."

"Two by two by two," the parrot proclaimed to the hippopotamus. "Noah wants pairs of every animal to enter the ark two by two."

The possums hanging in the treetops had nothing to say but "*Zzzz-Zzzz-Zzzz.*"

"We need our banana trees," said the swinging monkeys in the rain forest. "In forty days, we'll surely starve!"

"Don't worry," twittered the sparrows. "We'll have plenty to eat. Noah has promised us berries and nuts and fruits and grains. There will be honey and nectar, too."

And the birds spread the word across the lands both near and far, from the highest mountains to the Arctic shores.

"Food!" squawked the seagull. "The ark is filled with food enough for all!"

"Mmm!" roared the great white polar bears. "Let's hurry off this iceberg and go straight there!"

"Food!" rattled the kingfisher near the northern woodland caves.

"Great!" growled the grizzly bears. "Combs of wild honey are too good to resist."

The wild mustangs galloped across the desert plains.
They heard the news, too.

"Wild oats!" whinnied the mare. They ran to join
the others.

When the news spread to the marshlands, the elephants tossed their trunks high and trumpeted, "Hurrah!" And with their big strong legs, they *stomp-stomp-stomped* all the way to the ark.

The ground thundered with the pounding feet of wild beasts. The field mice heard it and scurried to meet the others. "Please, leave some seeds and grains for us!" they yipped.

"Berries and worms, too!" chirruped the robin redbreasts.

High up in the treetops, the squirrels chattered and barked. "Noah said we can feast on acorns while we travel on the ark!"

In the briar patches down below, the jackrabbits and hares heard the good news. "Sweet carrots and lettuce!" they twittered, and hopped happily on their way.

The growing parade trotted and trampled and flew their way toward the ark.

The tabby cats crouched in the fields and perked up their ears with delight. "Delicious milk and cream!" they purred.

But the possums dozed dreamily on. . . . *"Zzzz-Zzzz-Zzzz."*

Two by two they came, from the littlest of bugs to the biggest of bears, just as Noah had declared. Aardvarks, badgers, and Mongolian yaks; ermines and jaguars with spots on their backs; foxes, chipmunks, and kangaroos, too; ladybugs and butterflies bluer than blue; monkeys, moose, and raccoons with striped

tails; lions, llamas, peacocks, and quails; turkeys, turtles, and animals with horns, like rhinos, cows, and unicorns; dingoes, newts, spiders, and snails; great apes, and rabbits with big fluffy tails; waddling penguins, wriggly worms . . . they entered the ark in one massive swarm!

"Hurry!" urged Noah, for the skies were growing black. And the last of the herd—from warthogs to zebras—ran up the plank through the doors of the ark.

Father Noah checked his list and marked off each pair as the first crack of thunder drummed through the skies. "Oh, no!" he cried. "The possums are missing!" So the sharp-eyed eagles flew with great speed, and brought back the possums, who still were asleep. Then, as soon as Noah bolted the big door shut, the whole sky opened up . . . and it POURED, POURED, POURED!

The rains came down, down, down, and the waters rose up, up, up, until soon the ark floated higher than the tallest treetop. And down below, where birds once flew, swam schools of fish and a big shark, too!

The storm outside whipped the ark to and fro with the waves. Each rise and dip of the seesawing ark twisted and tangled the giraffes' necks in knots. The tigers felt seasick and moaned in despair.

The nighttime was the hardest for the chickens, chickadees, and hares. The mountain lions and foxes chased them. And the owls and the ospreys swooped low over their heads, keeping them awake the whole night.

But then in the morning when the predators tried to snooze, the rooster woke them with a *"Cock-a-doodle-doo!"*

The days were miserable for most everyone on board. The camels missed the feeling of the sand between their toes, and the flamingos had no water in which to wade. The antelope missed loping, and the beavers missed gnawing on wood. But the possums didn't miss a thing—they just snoozed and snoozed and snoozed.

On the fortieth night after the fortieth day, the heavens cleared
and at last the rain stopped. But the waters still covered the earth
as far as the eye could see. So God sent the winds to clear the
waters away. They drifted for days until . . . *BUMP!* The ark
landed on the tip of Mount Ararat.

When the winds stopped blowing and the ark stopped rocking, Noah opened the windows and looked all about. But all he saw was water, so he sent out a dove to scout for land. She flew far and wide and returned only to coo, "I'm tired and must rest. I could find no place to perch my feet or build myself a nest."

Seven days passed, and the animals grew restless and weary.
So Noah sent out the dove again and prayed that she'd return
in a hurry. The dove flew off, and to everyone's relief, she
returned with the gift of an olive branch in her beak.

"Land!" Noah shouted. "Praise be to God! Let's disembark
and let the animals run wild!"

Noah, his wife, and their sons, Shem, Ham, and Japheth, climbed down from the mountain and stepped foot on dry earth. The geese circled high, honking, "Home! Home! Home!" And the animals roamed to the far corners of the land to start up new families in forests, fields, snow, and sand.

God blessed Noah and his children and said, "Have many children, so that your descendants will live all over the earth. I promise you and all living things—all birds and all animals that came out of the ark with you—that a great flood will never come again."

ALICE was growing tired, listening to her sister read. Just as her eyes began to close, she saw a white rabbit hurry by, looking at his pocket watch and talking to himself. Alice thought that was very curious indeed—a talking rabbit with a pocket watch! So she followed him into a rabbit hole beneath a big tree.

And down she fell, down to the center of the world, it seemed.

When Alice landed with a thump, the White Rabbit was just disappearing through a door, which was much too small for her.

Alice drank from a bottle on the table and shrank down to a very tiny size. But now she could not reach the key to the little door!

DRINK ME

At last, Alice found a way to get through the little door. Seated on a bottle, she floated into Wonderland on a mysterious sea.

On the shore of the Wonderland Sea, Alice joined a race. It had no beginning; it had no end—you just ran around and around.

On through Wonderland Alice went, in search of the White Rabbit. She met two jolly fellows, Tweedledum and Tweedledee.

They did not know the rabbit, but they told Alice a wonderful story about a walrus and a carpenter who walked beside the sea.

Alice listened politely. Then she hurried on. And finally, at a neat little house in the woods, she met the White Rabbit himself! The rabbit sent Alice into his little house to hunt for his gloves. But instead she found some cookies labeled TAKE ONE. So she did.

The cookie made Alice grow as big as the house! The White
Rabbit and his friend Dodo thought she was a dreadful monster.
Alice picked a carrot from the rabbit's garden. Eating it made her
small again—so small that she was soon lost in a forest of grass.

Soon Alice found herself in a garden of live, talking flowers. There were bread-and-butterflies and rocking-horseflies, too. Alice thought the garden was a pleasant place. But the flowers

thought Alice was just a weed, so they would not let her stay.

Next, Alice met a haughty caterpillar. He told her to eat the mushroom that he was sitting on if she wished to change her size.

Alice sampled one side of the mushroom and shot up taller than the treetops, frightening the birds. But another bite made her just the right size.

"Now, which way shall I go?" Alice wondered. The signposts she found along the path were no help—they pointed in every direction.

"If I were looking for the White Rabbit, I'd ask the Mad Hatter," said a grinning Cheshire Cat up in a tree. "He lives down there."

Alice found the Mad Hatter and the March Hare celebrating their un-birthdays at a tea party. She joined them for a while.

After that nonsensical tea party, Alice wanted to go home. But none of the strange creatures she met seemed to know the way.

Alice wandered into the Queen's Garden. But the gardeners could not help her. They were all busy as could be, painting the roses red. Then along came the Royal Procession. And who should be the royal trumpeter for the Queen of Hearts but the White Rabbit himself!

The Queen asked Alice to play croquet. But Alice did not like the looks of the game. "Off with her head!" cried the Queen. Away Alice ran, while the army of cards chased her, down all the tangled paths of Wonderland, and back to the riverbank.

"I'm glad to be back where things are really what they seem,"
said Alice as she woke up from her strange Wonderland dream.

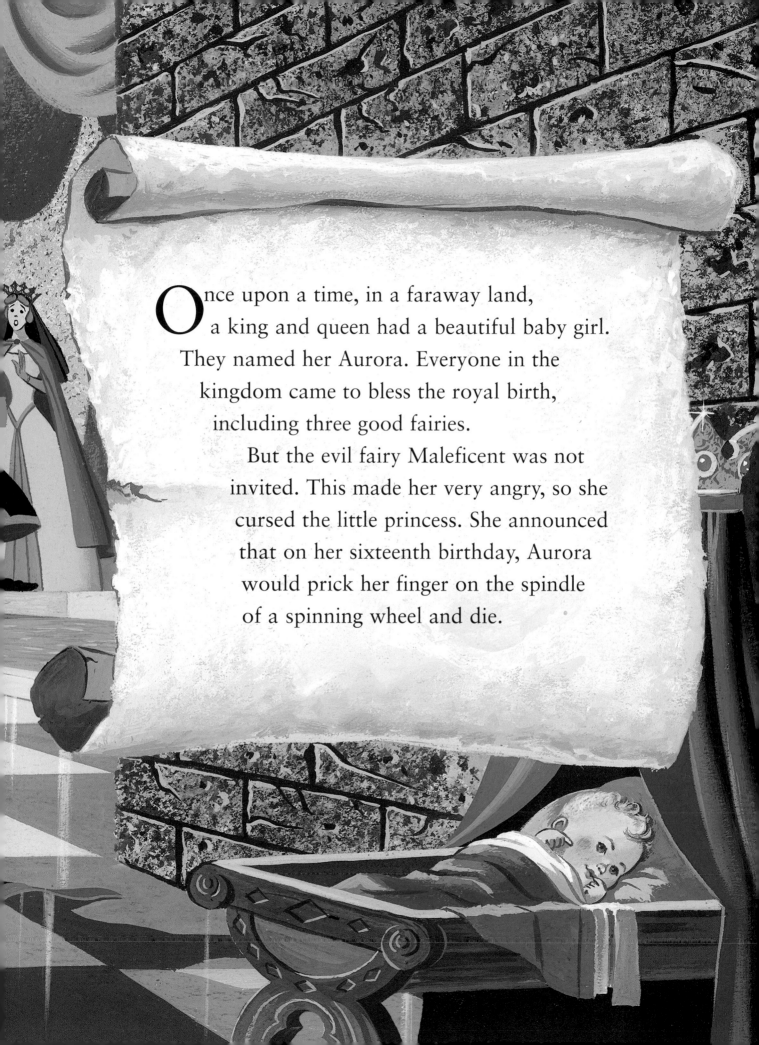

Once upon a time, in a faraway land,
a king and queen had a beautiful baby girl.
They named her Aurora. Everyone in the
kingdom came to bless the royal birth,
including three good fairies.

But the evil fairy Maleficent was not
invited. This made her very angry, so she
cursed the little princess. She announced
that on her sixteenth birthday, Aurora
would prick her finger on the spindle
of a spinning wheel and die.

The king and queen were horrified. But the good
fairies, Flora, Fauna, and Merryweather, came up with
a plan to protect Princess Aurora from Maleficent.

They disguised themselves as peasants and raised Aurora deep
in the woods. To be extra safe, the fairies agreed to stop using
magic so that no one—especially Maleficent—would be suspicious.

Sixteen years went by, and no one discovered
Aurora's secret home. Her only companions were
the birds and fluffy-tailed squirrels and rabbits.

But the princess was never lonely, for she played
with her animal friends every day. She sang to them,
and told them about her dreams of falling in love.

On Princess Aurora's sixteenth birthday, her dreams came true! Prince Phillip heard a beautiful song in the forest and followed the sound. He came upon a clearing and found Aurora, singing. They fell in love at first sight. All Aurora's forest friends shared in their joy as the happy couple danced and danced.

Meanwhile, the fairies were planning a secret birthday surprise for Aurora. Fauna tried to whip up a fancy layer cake. She opened a recipe book and started mixing all the ingredients in a big bowl.

Flora wanted to make Aurora an extra special dress.
She used Merryweather as a model. First, Flora cut a hole
in the center of the cloth for Aurora's head to fit through!

Poor Fauna didn't know the first thing about making a cake. She tried and tried and tried, but the only thing she could make was a gooey mess.

And Flora had never made a dress before. She snipped and clipped here and pinned and patched there, but she only succeeded in making Merryweather cry. Flora had stitched together a gown absolutely unfit for a princess.

Merryweather finally had enough of Flora and Fauna's nonsense. After sixteen years, it was time to get out their wands. They needed magic to clean up their mess! So, with a few simple whisks of their wands . . . Fauna's cake rose to perfection with pink icing and brilliant candles.

And Flora's fabric gathered itself, trimmed itself, and
sewed itself together. With a wave of her wand, it became
a lovely pink gown. Oh, no, thought Merryweather, that
won't do. And in the blink of an eye, she changed the
gown's color to a brilliant blue.

The fairies brought Aurora back to the
castle on the evening of her sixteenth birthday.
Everyone at the palace eagerly awaited her
return. But the wicked Maleficent also came
to the castle and waited for the princess.
She lured Aurora to the top of a tower
where she saw a magic spinning wheel.
Then, Maleficent's horrible curse was
fulfilled. The princess touched the spindle
and pricked her finger.

The princess fell to the floor. The fairies wept, for they couldn't stop Maleficent. But Aurora didn't die. The good fairies had worked their magic so that the princess simply fell into a deep sleep. She would awaken only after the first kiss from her true love.

Flora, Fauna, and Merryweather couldn't bear to break the king's heart with the news of Aurora's fate. So they made everyone else in the castle fall asleep, too—all the guards, the ladies-in-waiting, even the king and queen.

Once the palace was totally quiet, the fairies flew
away with magical speed. They needed to find the
handsome prince who would break the spell.

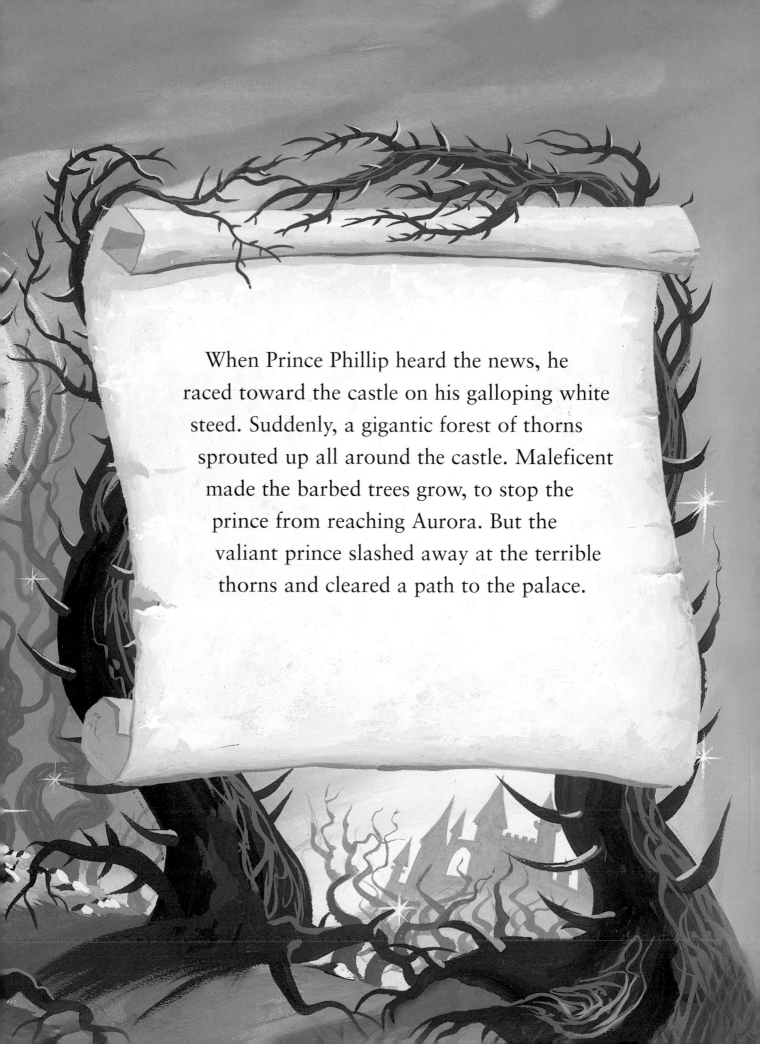

When Prince Phillip heard the news, he raced toward the castle on his galloping white steed. Suddenly, a gigantic forest of thorns sprouted up all around the castle. Maleficent made the barbed trees grow, to stop the prince from reaching Aurora. But the valiant prince slashed away at the terrible thorns and cleared a path to the palace.

As soon as the prince got to the palace, a fierce and furious
dragon appeared before him. It was Maleficent, who used all
her powers to transform herself into a fire-breathing dragon!
The dragon blasted Phillip with a fierce blaze.

The prince stumbled back and nearly fell off a cliff.
But using all his strength, he held up his shield and hurled
his mighty sword deep into the heart of the dragon. The
monstrous Maleficent was slain, once and for all!

The prince dashed to Aurora's side and gave her a kiss. The princess began to stir. Her eyelids fluttered open, and she awoke at last! Happiness filled her heart when she saw her handsome prince.

Then, the fairies' spell lifted, as one by one, the king and queen and everyone else awoke from their slumber, yawning and stretching.

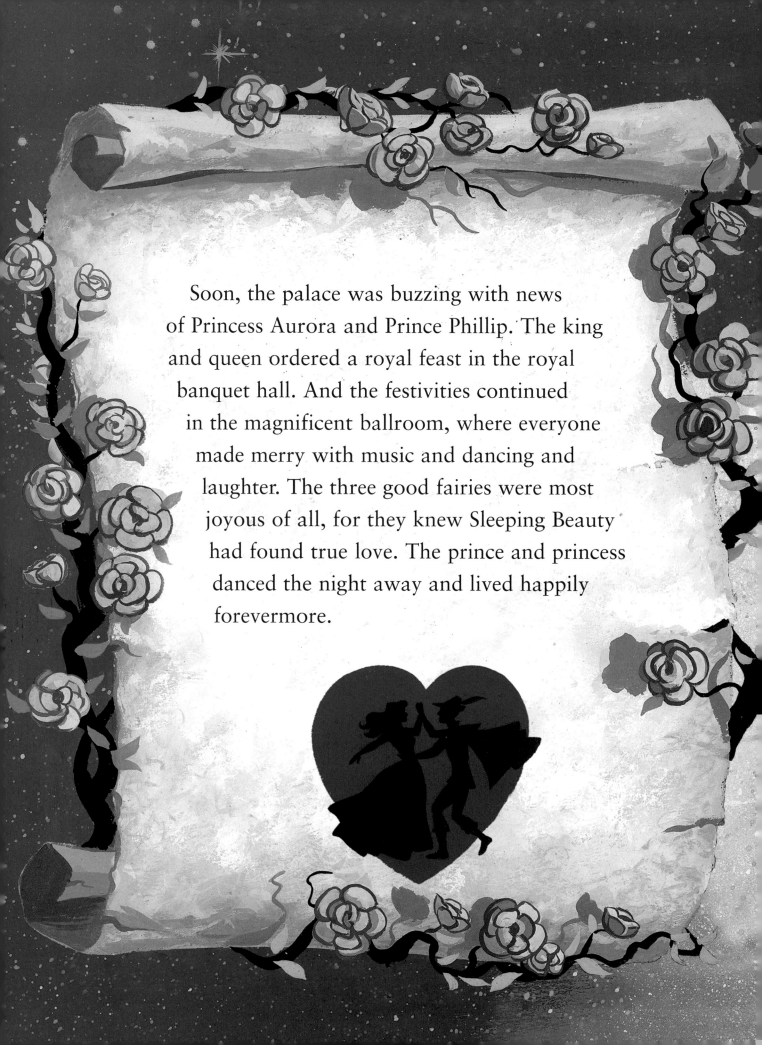

Soon, the palace was buzzing with news
of Princess Aurora and Prince Phillip. The king
and queen ordered a royal feast in the royal
banquet hall. And the festivities continued
in the magnificent ballroom, where everyone
made merry with music and dancing and
laughter. The three good fairies were most
joyous of all, for they knew Sleeping Beauty
had found true love. The prince and princess
danced the night away and lived happily
forevermore.

Walt Disney's

DUMBO

It was spring—springtime in the circus! After the long winter's rest, it was time to set out again on the open road, and everyone was eager to go.

"*Toot! Toot!*" whistled Casey Junior, the locomotive of the circus train.

"All aboard!" shouted the Ringmaster.

The acrobats, the jugglers, the tumblers, and the snake charmers scrambled to their places on the train. The keepers locked the animal cages. Then, with a jiggety jerk and a brisk *puff-puff*, off sped Casey Junior. The circus was on its way!

→≫≫ TO THE CIRCUS →

Everyone was happy. All the mother animals had new babies to love. All but Mrs. Jumbo. Her baby elephant had not yet arrived, and she wondered how the stork would ever find her.

But what was this? A special-delivery stork was flying after the circus train. "Mrs. Jumbo? Where is Mrs. Jumbo?" he asked.

Eventually, the stork found the elephant car and left his precious bundle at Mrs. Jumbo's side.

All the other elephants were waiting to see the new baby. And what a darling, chubby baby elephant he was.

"Koochie-koo, little Jumbo, koochie-koo!" said one of the grown-ups as she tickled the baby under his chin.

The tickling made him sneeze. And when he sneezed, out flapped his enormous ears! The biggest ears any elephant had ever seen!

"He'll never be a little Jumbo." The grown-ups laughed. "Little Dumbo is the name for him!"

Poor little Dumbo toddled to his mother, and tenderly she rocked him to sleep in her trunk.

Before morning dawned, Casey Junior brought the train to a stop in the city where the circus was to open that day. Then the circus folk got ready for the big parade.

Down the main street pranced the gay procession. There were cream-white horses and licorice-colored seals. There were lady acrobats in pink silk tights and lions pacing in their gilded wagon-cages, and last but not least came the elephants marching slowly, in single file.

At the end of the line came little Dumbo. "Look at that silly animal with the draggy ears!" cried the crowd. "He can't be an elephant! He must be a clown!"

Dumbo, toddling along behind his mother with his trunk clasped around her tail, tried to hurry faster so he wouldn't hear the laughter. But alas, he stumbled and tripped on his ears. Down he went in a puddle of mud. The crowd roared with laughter at the baby elephant.

Back in the tent, Mrs. Jumbo gave Dumbo a bath so that he would look fine for the first show that afternoon. Then, they ate their lunch and went to their stalls in the menagerie.

Soon the crowd was streaming through the tents. A group of boys gathered near the rope in front of Mrs. Jumbo's stall. "We want to see the baby elephant!" they yelled. "The one with the sailboat ears!"

A boy grabbed one of Dumbo's ears and pulled it, hard. Then he made an ugly face and stuck out his tongue.

Mrs. Jumbo could not stand to see Dumbo being teased. She reached out with her trunk, snatched the boy up, dropped him across the rope, and spanked him.

"Help, help!" he cried. And then the keepers arrived.

Mrs. Jumbo reared on her hind legs. But soon she was behind the bars in the prison wagon with a big sign above her that said DANGER! MAD ELEPHANT! KEEP OUT!

Worst of all, the other elephants would have nothing to do with Dumbo. They even turned their backs on him in a solid wall.

Now, hidden in the hay pile was Timothy Mouse, the circus mouse. Timothy loved scaring elephants, and he thought this was the best time to do it.

"They can't treat the little fellow that way," he muttered.

So, Timothy stepped out. "Boo! Boo!" he yelled. And the big brave elephants ran in all directions, leaving Timothy and Dumbo alone.

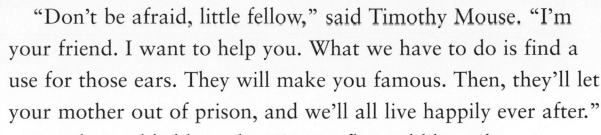

"Don't be afraid, little fellow," said Timothy Mouse. "I'm your friend. I want to help you. What we have to do is find a use for those ears. They will make you famous. Then, they'll let your mother out of prison, and we'll all live happily ever after."

Dumbo nodded happily. His ears flapped like sails.

"I've got it!" Timothy shouted. "You know the big-elephant balancing act at the end of the show? Well, when they have their pyramid built, you'll jump on the acrobats' springboard and bounce right up to the top of that pyramid, waving a little flag. You'll be the star of the show. Let's sneak out and practice now!"

On their way to the practice field, they passed the prison wagon where Mrs. Jumbo stood, sadly staring out into the night.

How delighted she was to see her baby. And how happy Dumbo was to curl up safe in the curve of his mother's trunk once more.

He told her all about the elephant act, about how unhappy he was without her, and about the wonderful idea Timothy had for making him a success.

Finally, Timothy had to pull Dumbo away, so that they could practice springboard jumping.

When Dumbo could jump from the springboard to a stand twenty feet high, Timothy whispered his idea into the sleeping Ringmaster's ear. And the very next day, as a surprise, Dumbo's jump was added as a highlight to the show.

The great moment came. The pyramid of elephants was swaying in the ring. Dumbo ran down the springboard. Then it happened. He tripped over his flapping ears! Up he bounced, in a twirling ball, and he crashed into that great pyramid of elephants, knocking them in every direction at once!

The next day, they made Dumbo into a clown. They painted his face with a foolish grin and dressed him in a baby dress. On his head they put a bonnet. And they used him in the most ridiculous act in the show—a make-believe fire. Dumbo had to jump from the top of a blazing cardboard house, down into the clown-firemen's net. The audience thought it was a great joke. But Dumbo felt terrible. And he was frightened, too.

"Don't worry, Dumbo," Timothy whispered as he curled up in Dumbo's hat brim. "We'll have you starring in the show yet. You'll be flying high!"

Back in the circus tent, Dumbo fell asleep at once, and he dreamed a beautiful dream. He was the star of a magical circus—a circus the likes of which had never been seen before. In the dream there was a springboard, spotlighted in the center of the tent. Dumbo himself, dressed in a gorgeous costume, stepped onto the springboard, bounced high into the air—and then away he flew.

It seemed as easy as anything, and very, very real.

The next morning, Timothy was the first to awaken.
Close beside him, three black crows sat and stared at him.
"What are *you* doing here?" Timothy asked sleepily.
"What are you doing here?" snapped the crows.
At that, Timothy sat up and took another look around
him. "Why—why, where am I?" he gasped. He was still
in the brim of Dumbo's hat, and the hat was still on top
of Dumbo's head. But Dumbo was asleep on the branch
of a tree far, far above the ground!

"How did we get here?" Timothy asked.

"Flew!" the crows cackled.

"Flying?" yelled Timothy. "Dumbo, Dumbo, you flew!"

Slowly Dumbo opened his eyes. He glanced down. He gulped. Then he struggled to his feet. He tried to balance in the wobbly tree fork, but he slipped . . . down, down, down! He bounced from branch to branch, with Timothy clinging on for dear life. *Plonk!* They landed in a brook beneath the tree. The crows chuckled and cawed from above.

Timothy scrambled up out of the water. "Dumbo!" he cried. "You can fly! If you can fly when you're asleep, you can fly when you're awake." So Dumbo tried again . . . and again. . . . But he could not leave the ground.

With Timothy as his teacher, Dumbo practiced for hours. He ran and he jumped and he hopped—and he tripped. He tried fast and slow takeoffs. He tried standing and running jumps. He counted as he flapped his ears—one, two, three, four. But as hard as he tried, Dumbo could not fly.

At last, the crows felt sorry for him. "Here, try this magic feather," one of them said. "This is how we teach our babies to fly. Hold onto this and you'll be fine."

Dumbo clutched the feather in the tip of his trunk, and he tried once more. The magic-feather trick worked like a charm. No sooner had Dumbo wrapped his trunk around the feather than *flap, flap, flap* went his ears. Up into the air he soared like a bird. He glided, he dipped, and he dived. And he circled over the heads of the cheering crows.

Then he headed back to the circus grounds, with Timothy cheering as loud as he could.

"We must keep your flying a secret—a surprise for this afternoon's show," Timothy decided. So they landed before they reached the tents.

When they got back safely, without being missed, it was time for Dumbo to get into his costume for the big clown act.

Then he had to wait inside the little cardboard house until make-believe fire crackled up around him. But today he did not mind. Because Timothy was with him.

Cr-rr-rr-ack! Cr-rr-ack! crackled the fire. *Clang! Clang!* roared the clown fire engine, rushing toward the blaze.

"Save my baby!" cried a clown, dressed up as a mother. That was Dumbo's cue to appear at the window. So Timothy tucked the magic feather into the curve of his trunk, and climbed up to his place in Dumbo's hat brim.

"Good luck, Dumbo!" he cried.

The firemen brought a big net and held it out.

"Jump, my baby, jump!" shrieked the mother clown.

Dumbo jumped, but as he did, the magic feather slipped and floated away. Now my magic is gone, Dumbo thought.

He plunged down like a stone.

Timothy saw the feather drift past. He knew how Dumbo felt. "It's all right, Dumbo!" he shouted. "The feather was a trick! You can fly by yourself!"

Dumbo heard the shout. Doubtfully, he spread his ears wide. Just two feet above the firemen's net, he stopped his plunge and swooped up into the air!

A mighty gasp arose from the audience. They knew it couldn't be . . . but it was! Dumbo was flying!

While the crowd roared with delight, Dumbo did power dives, loops, spins, and barrel rolls. He swooped down to pick up peanuts and squirted a trunkful of water on the clowns.

The keepers freed Mrs. Jumbo and brought her to see her baby fly. Now all Dumbo's worries were over.

Soon, Dumbo was a hero from coast to coast. Timothy became his manager and arranged a wonderful contract for Dumbo with a big salary and a pension for his mother.

The circus was renamed Dumbo's Flying Circus, and Dumbo traveled in a special streamlined car.

But best of all, he forgave everyone who had been unkind to him, for his heart was as big as his magical ears.

Walt Disney's
The Ugly Duckling

In the heart of the beautiful countryside lived a mother duck. Her nest was in the loveliest spot under a big, shady tree. She longed to stretch her legs and go for a swim in the warm summer sun. But instead she sat patiently, waiting for her five eggs to hatch.

After many long and quiet days, Mother Duck heard a pecking sound. Could it be time?

"*Quack! Quack!*" she cried and hopped off her nest to peek at the eggs. One wiggled. Another wobbled. The pecking sounds got louder and louder. *Crack-crack-crack-crack!* Out popped one . . . two . . . three . . . *four* fuzzy ducklings!

The downy youngsters scrambled out of their shells as quickly as their webbed feet could waddle. "Look how big and bright the world is!" they peeped as they explored all around their nest.

"The world is far bigger than this, my children." Mother Duck smiled. "Follow me, and we'll go for a refreshing swim in the lake."

Before she could lead her ducklings to the water, Mother Duck remembered the fifth egg. "Oh, dear!" she cried. "The biggest egg of all still hasn't hatched. Hmph!" she snorted grumpily.

"It's probably a turkey egg," she muttered.
"Oh, well, I sat this long. I might as well sit a bit
longer." And so, Mother Duck settled back down
on the biggest egg.

Finally, after a very long time, the big egg began to wiggle and wobble. Mother Duck and her precious ducklings gathered around the nest to watch. At last, *crrrrack!* The new hatchling broke out of his shell!

What a sight he was! He looked nothing like his brothers and sisters. Instead of being sunshiny yellow, he was a dull gray. And he was awfully big.

"*Honk! Honk!*" he greeted his new family.

But his brothers and sisters weren't so friendly.

"You're *ugly*!" quacked the ducklings.

"Yes," agreed Mother Duck. "You must be a turkey, after all. All my other children are the spitting image of their father." Then Mother Duck turned her back on the big hatchling and quacked to the others. "Come along, children, we've waited long enough to go for a swim."

"*Quack! Quack! Quack!*" piped the youngsters. "We don't want to swim with such an ugly duckling!"

The Ugly Duckling wanted to swim, too. He followed the others to the lake and floated easily on the surface. The cool water felt so refreshing on his big, floppy feet!

"Look, Mom! I can swim, too!" he called. But Mother Duck and the ducklings swam away and pretended not to notice him.

So the Ugly Duckling found himself all alone on the big lake. Heartbroken, he swam to a quiet spot among the marshy reeds. There, hidden from the rest of the world, the poor duckling drooped his head and cried and cried and cried. Big, sad tears splashed into the lake.

As the Ugly Duckling looked at the ripples each teardrop made in the water, he saw a horrible sight—a terrible, twisted face looking right back at him. It was his own reflection.

"I *am* ugly!" he cried. "No wonder no one wants to be near me!" And he covered his eyes from his image and felt more alone than before.

The Ugly Duckling decided to run far, far away where no
one would be bothered by his ugliness. He waddled through
fields and glens, deep into the forest.

Finally, he came upon a clearing where he saw a nest of young birds chirping happily away.

Maybe they'll be my friends, he thought. And for the first time, he felt hopeful.

The Ugly Duckling climbed into the tree. *"Cheep, cheep, cheep, cheep!"* the baby birds greeted him. "Come play with us. Mother is returning soon with food. She'll be happy to have you in our nest."

"Thank you!" honked the Ugly Duckling. How wonderful it would be to have a mother who would welcome him! He played with his new brothers and sisters and waited patiently for Mother Bird.

Soon, Mother Bird came home with a fat, juicy worm in her mouth. The Ugly Duckling had forgotten how hungry he was and snapped the worm right out of Mother Bird's beak and swallowed it whole.

"*Squawk, squawk, squawk!*" scolded Mother Bird. "Shame on you, you big ugly thing! How dare you take food away from my babies!" And she shooed him out of her nest and far away from her children.

The Ugly Duckling had to keep running so he wouldn't get snapped in the tail by the angry mother bird.

The Ugly Duckling wandered for many lonely hours until he came to a large pond.

There, floating among the reeds, he saw the biggest, friendliest-looking duck he had ever seen. "Perhaps he won't mind that I'm so ugly," he said hopefully. So he swam timidly toward the colorful mallard.

The big duck didn't swim away or call him names! He simply smiled warmly.

The Ugly Duckling snuggled close to his newfound friend. He was so overcome with happiness, he didn't even notice that the mallard wasn't a duck at all. He was nothing more than painted wood.

The Ugly Duckling nudged the smiling decoy. "Let's play!" he honked.

The wooden duck bobbed his head up and down and up and down.

"At last! Someone wants to play with me!" cried the Ugly Duckling. Excited, he climbed onto the big duck's back and jumped into the water. *Splash!* What fun!

And he continued to splash and play, filling the pond with waves. The decoy bobbed back and forth more and more until . . . *BONK!* Its big, wooden bill hit the Ugly Duckling smack-dab in the middle of his forehead!

The Ugly Duckling paddled to safety as quickly as he could. "He must have attacked me because I'm so ugly!" he wailed.

Then the sad little duckling suddenly realized he would have to spend the rest of his life all alone. The thought hurt him more than a bump on his head ever could. And he flopped on the log and cried his little heart out.

Out of the blue, he heard a *honk-honk-honking* all around him. He looked up and saw the most wonderful sight of all—a flock of magnificent young birds gathered around him!

He thought they were the loveliest creatures he'd ever seen. If only he could be half as lovely!

He was so elated to have company that he dove all the way to the bottom of the pond.

But when he popped up at the surface, he found himself alone once again.

The other birds were paddling away, *honk-honk-honking* in the distance.

Why should I think that they would want to play with me? he thought gloomily.

Just when he thought he would be alone and miserable forever, something amazing happened! The beautiful birds returned. And with them swam the most glorious bird in the world.

"Look, Mother!" honked the happy cygnets. "We've found a new brother!"

The Ugly Duckling couldn't believe his eyes or his ears.

"You're home, now, little one," said the mother swan as she cradled the Ugly Duckling under her snowy-white wing. "You are a fine young swan."

From the shore, Mother Duck and her ducklings watched the graceful swan welcome the Ugly Duckling into her family.

As he swam away with his new family, he ruffled his feathers and held his head up high. Never before had the Ugly Duckling felt so much love in his heart.